John D. MacDonald and The Murder Room

>>> This title is part of The Murder Room, our series dedicated to making available out-of-print or hard-to-find titles by classic crime writers.

Crime fiction has always held up a mirror to society. The Victorians were fascinated by sensational murder and the emerging science of detection; now we are obsessed with the forensic detail of violent death. And no other genre has so captivated and enthralled readers.

Vast troves of classic crime writing have for a long time been unavailable to all but the most dedicated frequenters of second-hand bookshops. The advent of digital publishing means that we are now able to bring you the backlists of a huge range of titles by classic and contemporary crime writers, some of which have been out of print for decades.

From the genteel amateur private eyes of the Golden Age and the femmes fatales of pulp fiction, to the morally ambiguous hard-boiled detectives of mid twentieth-century America and their descendants who walk our twenty-first century streets, The Murder Room has it all. **>>>**

The Murder Room
Where Criminal Minds Meet

themurderroom.com

T0373049

John D. MacDonald (1916–1986)

John D. MacDonald was born in Pennsylvania and married Dorothy Prentiss in 1937, graduating from Syracuse University the following year and receiving an MBA from Harvard in 1939. It was Dorothy who was responsible for the publication of his first work, when she submitted a short story that he had sent home while on military service. It was initially rejected by *Esquire* but went on to be published by *Story* magazine – and so began MacDonald's writing career. One of the best-loved and most successful of all the masters of hard-boiled crime and suspense, John D. Macdonald was producing brilliant fiction long after many of his contemporaries had been forgotten, and is still highly regarded today. *The Executioners*, possibly the best known of his non-series novels, was filmed as *Cape Fear* in 1962 and 1991, but many of the crime thrillers he produced between 1953 and 1964 are considered masterpieces, and he drew praise from such literary luminaries as Kurt Vonnegut and Stephen King, who declared him to be '*the* great entertainer of our age, and a mesmerizing storyteller'. His novels are often set in his adopted home of Florida, including those featuring his famous series character Travis McGee, which appeared between 1964 and 1985. He served as president of the Mystery Writers of America and in 1972 was elected a Grand Master, an honour granted only to the greatest crime writers of their generation, including Ross MacDonald, John Le Carré and P. D. James. He won many awards throughout his long career, and was the only mystery writer ever to win the National Book Award, for *The Green Ripper*.

By John D. MacDonald
(published in The Murder Room)

The Brass Cupcake (1950)
Murder for the Bride (1951)
The Neon Jungle (1953)
Cancel All Our Vows (1953)
Area of Suspicion (1954)
Contrary Pleasure (1954)
A Bullet for Cinderella (1955)
   (aka On the Make)
Cry Hard, Cry Fast (1956)
April Evil (1956)
Border Town Girl (1956)
   (aka Five Star Fugitive)
Hurricane (1956)
   (aka Murder in the Wind)
You Live Once (1956)
   (aka You Kill Me)
Death Trap (1957)
The Price of Murder (1957)
A Man of Affairs (1957)
The Deceivers (1958)
Soft Touch (1958)
Deadly Welcome (1959)
The Beach Girls (1959)
Please Write for Details
   (1959)

The Crossroads (1959)
Slam the Big Door (1960)
The Only Girl in the Game
   (1960)
The End of the Night (1960)
Where is Janice Gantry? (1961)
One Monday We Killed Them
   All (1961)
A Key to the Suite (1962)
A Flash of Green (1962)
I Could Go On Singing
   (screenplay novelisation)
   (1963)
On the Run (1963)
The Drowner (1963)
The Last One Left (1966)
No Deadly Drug (1968)
One More Sunday (1984)
Barrier Island (1986)

Collections

The Good Old Stuff (1961)
Seven (1971)
More Good Old Stuff (1984)

Murder for the Bride

John D. MacDonald

Chapter One

IT WAS one of those days when everything goes wrong. I should have guessed that the letter would mean trouble.

Paul Harrigan and I had been working in a swamp for the six weeks following my three-day honeymoon with Laura. It was a juicy Mexican swamp five miles west of Tancoco, about a hundred miles south of Tampico. Trans-Americas Oil, our employer, had a contract with Permex of Mexico to find, or try to find, new oil reserves. On the basis of aerial photo maps, Sam Spencer had shoved two-man crews into the more promising spots to bounce echoes off the substrata and map in detail any promising-looking domes. It's a simple operation in open country. Harrigan and I were given a swamp. Every inch of the way had to be hacked out, and the equipment had to be lugged by hand.

It was one of those days. It seemed even hotter than usual, the clouds of insects shriller and hungrier, the black muck stickier. Wild parrots in their clown suits made noises like a fingernail on a blackboard, and even the orchids looked like open wounds.

One of the labor gang chopped his leg instead of a vine. We got the bleeding stopped and built a litter and sent him on back along the trail to Tancoco with instructions to Fernando, our base-camp man, to send him in the truck down to the doctor in Tuxpan. Later Harrigan made a check with the compass and advised the world at large in a profane bellow that the most recent trail wandered off in the wrong direction.

Sam Spencer was using the mails to ride us about the

1

time we were taking. He didn't want us to finish any more badly than I wanted to be done with it and get back to Laura. I had begun to think at thirty-two that marriage was for the other boys, not for me. There had been girls aplenty, but it had reached the serious stages with no more than three—and even then there had been something missing. With Laura there was nothing missing. It was all there. And to hell with what other people thought of my Laura. We met right after I got back to New Orleans after six months in Venezuela. We were married that same week.

Harrigan was having a bad time with me. I did everything except walk into trees and talk to myself. Every time I shut my eyes I could see her silver-blonde hair, jet eyebrows, sooty smudge of lashes, sherry-brown eyes. I could remember so clearly the feel of her in my arms, the sting of those pouting, arrogant lips, every line of her tall, warm, wonderful figure. Laura Rentane—now Mrs. Dillon Bryant.

We were just getting back to work after the noon break when the boy came from the base camp with the mail. Two letters. One to Paul Harrigan from Spencer. One to me, on *New Orleans Star News* stationery, with Jill Townsend's name typed in under the printing on the top left corner.

Whenever Sam Spencer used to call me back to New Orleans, I used to get in touch with Jill. We had a lot of laughs, a lot of fun. She's a little girl—the top of her dark head reaches no higher than my lips—but her slimness and the way she carries herself make her look taller. Her eyes are gray and sharp with intelligence, and her face is out of kilter in a funny way, the small chin canted a bit to the left, the left side of her mouth and her left eye set just about a millimeter higher than the features on the right side. It gives her a wonderfully wry look. The paper had her on society stuff for a long time before, in her spare time, she unraveled a particularly unpleasant smuggling angle, got her life threatened, got some people sent to one of Uncle Sam's jails, and got herself promoted.

When Laura and I were trying to cut the red tape to get married quickly, Jill helped us. Laura didn't seem to care much for Jill, and that annoyed me a little because Jill helped a lot with the papers and also with finding Laura a little apartment in the Quarter. Then I realized that Laura couldn't be expected to take a shine to someone classified as an ex among her new husband's old friends.

I tore the envelope open. The sticky heat of the swamp had dampened the paper so that you couldn't even hear it tear. My fingers left dark smudges on the paper. I wondered what on earth Jill was writing me about. I'd told her to keep an eye on Laura, if she could, because Laura didn't know anyone at all in town, and because, if you don't watch it, you can get tangled up with some pretty funny people who live in the Quarter.

"Dear Dil," it read. She had typed it. "I think you had better get on back here. Laura is in trouble. I can't find out just how bad it is, but without trying to alarm you too much, I think I can say it is probably the worst kind of trouble. I guess she should have gone to Mexico with you, Dil."

That's all there was. I stood and read it three times. I couldn't seem to get the meaning of it clear in my head.

I think I tried to laugh. All I did was make a sound as though somebody had just cut my throat.

Harrigan stopped growling at Sam Spencer's letter and stared at me. "What's with you?"

I opened my mouth and nothing came out. I handed him the letter and walked away and stood with my back to him. I got out a cigarette and got it lighted on the second try.

He came up behind me and put his hand on my shoulder. I skittered away from it like a nervous horse. "Easy, boy," he said.

"Oh, sure! Easy! What the hell, Paul!"

"You can take the jeep to Tuxpan and get an airplane ride to Mexico City. That will be the quickest."

"Leaving you holding the bag here."

"What good would you be? Dammit, Dil, why did you marry her without knowing anything about her?"

I turned on him. "Watch it, Paul!"

"Have I said a word so far? No. Now I'm talking, boy.

3

For your own good. Nobody could stop you. None of your friends. You had to go ahead and marry her. Women like that are always getting their hooks in the good guys."

"Paul!"

"Shut up. That Jill Townsend is tops. Everybody hoped it would be Jill. So did she, I think. I'm trying to prepare you, boy. I don't know what you're going to find up there. I do know it won't be pretty, whatever it is. Laura is an international tramp, boy, and the sooner . . ."

I saw my fist going out as if it belonged to somebody standing behind me. A big hard brown fist, with a hundred and ninety pounds behind it. Big Paul Harrigan is my height, six-one, but he outweighs me by thirty pounds. My fist went out as though in slow motion and I saw him just shut his eyes and turn his face a little and take it. It made a sound like hitting a wall with a wet rag. He went back lifting his arms to catch his balance, not quite making it, falling on hip and elbow. He sat up and there was blood on his mouth.

"I had to, Paul," I said, as if I were begging him for something. "I had to!"

"A woman like that," he said heavily, contemptuously. "A hard-eyed, sullen, discontented little . . ."

"Shut up!" I yelled. "You keep on and I'll hit you again, even if you are sitting down. She isn't like that, I tell you. You got her wrong, Paul. All wrong."

He got up. He rubbed his mouth with the back of his hand, then looked at the bright smear of blood. He sighed. "O.K., boy," he said. "I was asking for trouble. Come on. I'll drive you so I can bring the jeep back."

"Fernando can . . ."

"I'll drive you."

We didn't talk. Paul drove hard and fast. Dust boiled up in a long cloud behind the jeep. I was wondering what trouble Laura could be in. I had wanted Laura to come to Mexico. She said she'd been out of the States too long. I pleaded with her and she said no. Jill found the apartment for her. On Rampart. Three rooms and a little porch with lacy ironwork.

At the little Tuxpan strip I lifted my bag out. I set it

4

down and put my hand out. I said, "I'm sorry, Paul."

He took my hand. His blue eyes crinkled as he grinned. "I've been slugged before and will be again. No harm done." He sobered. "Do me one thing, boy. If Jill says so, Laura is in trouble. Try to keep your own nose clean. You get too excited. Just think before you jump. Can you do that?"

"I'll try, Paul."

"Let me know, hey?"

"I'll let you know. I'll see Spencer soon as I can. Maybe he can replace me if this trouble is going to take too long to clear up."

The charter on the old AT was cheap. Maybe too cheap. Right after take-off the radio quit. The motor sounded on the verge of stuttering out all the way. It was not long before the Sierra Madre lifted up underneath us, and a good two hours before I saw Mexico City cradled in the hollow of the plateau, the volcanoes high and white beyond it, dwarfing the mountains south of the city.

I made my plane connections, got my papers stamped, checked with the American consul, and got to the airport with minutes to spare. My flight stopped at Monterrey and went on to San Antonio. The flight from San Antonio left at dawn. I hadn't slept. I'd shaved in the men's room and changed to a rumpled white suit. I kept wishing Jill had told me more. Trouble isn't much of a word to go on. It can mean almost anything.

We came down out of the overcast over Lake Pontchartrain, passed the Air Force base, and let down into a still and breathless heat on a long strip at New Orleans Municipal. I grabbed a cab operated by a hairy little man and told him that I wanted speed. He made the turn onto Elysian Fields Avenue on two wheels and roared down through the morning traffic, hunched over the wheel, grinning like a fool. He gave the turn onto Rampart the same treatment and skidded to a shuddering halt right in front of the doorway. I gave him a five and waved away the change.

I gave one glance up at the little balcony and went up the stairs to the third floor, three at a time. I was calling

5

her name before I got my head above the floor level. I stopped calling when I saw the little man.

Three apartments opened off the top hallway. Pale light came from a dirty skylight over the stair well. The little man was standing leaning against the wall near Laura's apartment. I took the key out of my pocket and dropped my bag. For six weeks whenever I'd reached in my pocket and felt the key I'd thought of putting it in the lock and of Laura running toward me across the room, into my arms. The little man had a dusty-looking face, a dingy gray suit, an open collar, a straw hat shoved back off his forehead. He had a toothpick in the corner of his mouth. Soaking wet he might have weighed 130, gray suit and all.

Just as I shoved the key toward the lock he said in a mild tired voice, "Hold it, son."

"What's your trouble?" I demanded.

"You Bryant?"

"Yes. If you don't mind, I . . ."

"Can't go in there, son. Sorry."

I took two steps over to him and glared down at him. "And just why can't I go in there?"

"It's sealed. Police orders."

"Where's my wife?" Marriage was so new that the word "wife" felt strange on my lips.

He bobbled his toothpick over into the other corner of his mouth. I saw that his eyes were a funny color—like still water, like nail heads. I heard heavy steps coming up the stairs.

"Your wife is dead, son," he said in a tired and gentle voice. The world stopped turning and the sun stood still in the sky. I turned away from him. A uniformed police-man with a long sharp-featured face came into sight. Funny how every sense becomes so sharp at a time like that. The look of a long crack in the plaster engraved itself in the back of my brain. A mosquito had been mashed beside the crack. Maybe Laura had killed it. I could smell dust, varnish, dampness. I heard horns blaring at some distant traffic tie-up, soap-opera organ music on a radio on one of the floors below. I could hear the slow thud of my heart, the roar of blood in my ears, a tiny creak of belt leather as I breathed. Laura had ceased breathing. There was no more warmth to Laura. The long lovely legs were still.

I leaned my forehead against the rough plaster. I hit the plaster very, very gently with my fist in time to the thud of my heart. The knuckles were still a bit swollen from hitting Paul a thousand miles away.

"When? How?" I asked without turning. I whispered it, the way you tiptoe into a room where the dead wait for burial.

"Last night, son. Somewhere around midnight, as near we can judge. Somebody slugged her, wrapped a wire coat hanger around her neck, and twisted it tight with a pair of pliers. We don't know who, yet. But I imagine we'll find out. Heard you were on your way, Bryant. Figured you'd come right here. Been waiting."

"Where is she?" I whispered.

"Police morgue. Been legally identified. You don't want to see her."

I turned then. "Yes, I do. There could be some mistake."

"It's not a good thing to remember, son."

"I want to see her."

We went down the stairs. I didn't notice until we got to the police sedan that he had carried my bag down. He opened the door and tossed the bag in. As he got behind the wheel he said, "I'm Zeck, son. Lieutenant Barney Zeck. Captain Paris is right anxious for a chat with you."

"Let's go see her first, Lieutenant."

The car was like an oven from sitting in the sun. But I didn't feel warm. There was a coldness in me that no sun would reach. This was the one trouble I hadn't thought of.

We went and looked at her. I made it out through the arch to the courtyard, where I was sick. Then we went to see Captain Paris. He was a big man, and he seemed to suffer badly in the heat. His white shirt stuck to his chest and there was heat rash all over his arms. His office had only one window. A fan on top of a file cabinet snarled as it turned from side to side, blowing stale hot air around the room.

7

We sat down and an old man with a bald head and a green eyeshade came in with a notebook and sharp pencils. He opened the book on the corner of the desk.

"I've been talking to Sam Spencer about you, Bryant. He thinks you're a good man. Maybe too quick on the trigger, but sound in your field. How come that floozy got you on the hook, Bryant?"

I leaned across the desk at him, trying to get my hands on him. Barney Zeck got hold of my belt and yanked me back into the chair.

"That's no way to act, son," Zeck said in his weary voice.

"Then tell him to watch his mouth."

Paris yawned and scrubbed at his prickly heat with his knuckles. "Let's pick it up from the beginning. You met her seven weeks or so ago. Middle of May. What were the circumstances of your meeting this woman?"

"What's that got to do with somebody murdering her?"

"Bryant, you just take that chip off your shoulder and be good. We want to find out who killed her, and we'll do it our way."

I slumped down in the chair and looked at my knuckles. "All right, Captain. I'd been back from Venezuela about four days. I was working at the Trans-Americas Oil offices in the Jefferson Building. Tram Widdmar, who owns the import-export business, was a friend of mine overseas during the war. Every time I'm in town we usually get together. The fifteenth of May was the hundredth anniversary of the founding of the Sanderson Steamship Lines. They had a big party that night at the Bayton Hotel. Tram had a cocktail party for a big group out at his house ahead of time. I went with Jill Townsend. I met Laura Rentane there. She had come in that morning on the Sanderson *Mobile* from Buenos Aires. Bill French, first officer of the *Mobile,* brought her to the party. I saw her and fell hard."

"Why?"

I glared at him. "Why does anybody fall for a girl? Even the way she looks now, you can tell how pretty she was."

"So you ditched the Townsend girl and leeched onto the Rentane woman?"

"No. A group of us went to dinner together. And then to the Bayton. While I was dancing with Laura we made a date for the next day. She told me she was living at the Bayton. After I got back to my room at the Willow House about three in the morning, I called her up. We met and went for a walk. We walked until dawn. Everything seemed to click. We got married on the eighteenth."

"Ever notice the scars on her face?"

"Yes. The little ones at her temples. She was in an accident once."

"I guess you could call age an accident. She put her age on the marriage-certificate application as twenty-four, Bryant. The doctor says thirty-five would be a better guess."

"You're crazy!"

"You were suckered. Somebody went through all her stuff with a comb, Bryant. There aren't any personal papers of any description left in that apartment. Nothing. All we've had to go on is what she put on that application. She wrote that she was born in Williamsport, Pennsylvania. We got the teletype back a while ago. No record."

"That doesn't mean anything."

"We'll be the judge of that. She had a funny accent. It didn't come from Williamsport."

"She lived abroad most of her life. That's why. She was as American as you are, Paris."

He pulled on his lip. "I was born in Toronto. Now we got another thing. Everything she owned is fairly new. A good bit of it was bought here. Everything else was purchased in Buenos Aires. Everything else."

I stood up. "I think you're wasting your time and mine too, Captain. Maybe it's too hot for you. Maybe you're bored. But I don't get the point in building a big mystery about some maniac who broke into the apartment and killed my wife."

"Maniac?" he said. "We happen to know that she has been scared green for the last week. Something scared her. We don't know what. We've got the word of a reliable

9

person for that. She had a chain put on the door of her apartment. The door wasn't forced. Whoever did it, she let him in. She knew him. And no thief made that search. Thieves don't dig around in jars of face cream and take the backs off pictures."

I sat down. Zeck said tiredly, "Somebody was after her, son. And she knew it. And they got her. It's that simple. So we got to know everything so we can find some motive. What do you know about her? Where did she go to school?"

"A private school in Switzerland," I said dully. "She never told me the name of it. Her parents died in a French airline crash three years ago. They left her a lot of money. She traveled for the last three years. She said that she hadn't had a very happy time until she met and married me, and that she didn't want to talk about the past because it made her sad. I should make out like nothing ever happened to her until she walked into Tram's house with Bill French."

"What did she tell you about the scar along her ribs?"

"She said she was a tomboy when she was little. She was climbing a tree and fell and hit a stub of a broken limb."

"The doctor says that scar is somewhere between one and three years old, Bryant. It's a knife wound. Somebody tried hard, but hit a rib and skidded off."

"How do you know it's a knife wound?"

"From an X-ray plate I was looking at at eight o'clock this morning. The point of the knife is still in the rib where it broke off."

I cupped my hands over my eyes. "It's all . . . so crazy!"

He leaned toward me. His face was suddenly intent. "We're waiting for word from the State Department, Bryant. She had to have a passport. It had to be in the name she was using—Laura Rentane. I've got a hunch there won't be any passport on record, that she came in on forged papers."

"Why do you think that?"

"She was awful anxious to get married, Bryant. Married to a nice sound local guy with a good reputation. Tossing her out of the country would be ten times as easy if she were single. Can you imagine what kind of an unholy stink you would make if they tried to deport her?"

"But that alone . . ."

"And did she have any good reason for refusing to go to Mexico with you? She might have had trouble getting a tourist card. Maybe whoever built her a passport didn't build a birth certificate to go with it."

"She wanted to get married because she was in love with me!"

"Because you're so pretty?" he asked mildly. "We want to find out who she was. Finding out will maybe lead to who killed her and why. So you think of any little personal habits she had that might be recognized by somebody. There was no picture of her in the apartment. You got a picture?"

I frowned. "No, there wasn't time. She promised to have one taken and mail it to me, but she didn't."

"Did she write you?"

I flushed. "Twice."

Paris leaned back and put his pudgy fingertips together. "A doll like that not owning a picture of herself. Enough creams and lotions to stock a department store, and no picture of herself. The hair was one of the best dye jobs I've ever seen."

"It was natural!"

"With those eyebrows and eyelashes? Don't be a stupe any more than you can help, Bryant. How about her habits?"

"I don't know what sort of thing you mean."

"Food, sleep, reading, likes and dislikes. Anything."

I flushed again. "It was a honeymoon, and a short one at that. We . . . ate at crazy hours. She liked to go for walks. She avoided fattening foods. I never saw her read anything. She laughed a lot."

"Nothing yet. Keep going."

"She could take cat naps at any time of day. She took a lot of baths and showers. Three and four a day. She said she always did that whenever she could. She could speak French and Spanish. She liked movies, but we only went to one. She said she'd see a lot of movies while I was

11

away. She adored the color yellow. She wanted to keep up the tan she got on the ship. She used to spend hours on herself. Hair, nails, that sort of thing. She did exercises, twisting and bending and turning. She didn't like . . ." I paused as I felt myself go red again.

"Keep talking. What didn't she like?"

"Clothes. She liked to have the rooms warm enough so she could go without clothes. It was sort of . . . hard to get used to."

"None of this is going to help much, Bryant. Can you think of anything she said that sounded funny, that possibly you didn't understand at the moment and it makes better sense now?"

"Only one thing," I said dubiously, "and maybe it's nothing. She had a nightmare. She was moaning. I woke her up. She said something in a language I couldn't understand, then switched to English. I asked her about it. She told me it must have been me doing the dreaming. We had a sort of spat about it. It sounded to me like German. She said that was silly because she couldn't speak German."

Chapter Two

JILL was sitting on a bench in the hall when I came out of Paris' office with Zeck. She wore a pale green cotton dress and carried a big white purse. She was hatless, as usual. She jumped up and came to me, quick concern on her face.

She slung the bag on her shoulder and folded her fingers around my wrists tightly. "Dil, I'm so sorry. I'm so terribly sorry."

I tried to smile at her. My eyes were stinging. She knew I couldn't speak and so she turned to Barney and said, "Let me take him off your hands for a while, Barney. The man needs food."

"We don't need him any more right now, Miss Townsend. Where'll you be staying, Bryant? They'll be through with the apartment by late afternoon, but I guess you wouldn't want to . . ."

"The apartment will be fine," I said.

"You can leave your bag right here. I'll drop it off. I got to go back there anyhow."

"Thanks."

He looked at me with those colorless eyes for a few seconds. "Take care, son," he said softly and ambled down the hall.

We walked a block to a restaurant and took a booth in the back. "Better have a drink, Dil," she said.

The waiter brought the bourbon. It went down and felt good. I reached over and lit her cigarette. "It seems funny," I said. "Like a dream. Like it isn't happening. I keep thinking she'll be in the apartment waiting for me, Jill."

"I know," she said softly.

"Like a wave. It flattens out and then comes back in a big crest and hits me. We had so little time together."

She put her small warm hand over mine. "Order another drink, Dil," she said.

I held my hands out, palms opposed, fingers spread. "I want the man who did it, Jill. He's mine. He's my baby. My hands want him so bad they burn."

"Don't think that way, Dil. Don't!"

"How can I help thinking that way? Yesterday I got your letter. Tell me how you came to write it, Jill. Tell me everything about that letter."

"After you eat. There's time. Eat first. Don't try to talk if you don't feel like it."

I ate three hungry forkfuls and then my throat seemed to close. I couldn't touch any more. I smoked and watched her eat. A little girl with a good healthy appetite. Now and then she'd smile at me. Just a smile that said we were friends. Paul was wrong. It had never been any other way between Jill and me. In her mind or mine.

The coffee came. We both took it sugarless and black.

"All right, Dil. Let me go all the way through it. Laura

13

didn't like me. You knew that. I don't think she liked
any woman, or was liked by any woman. I didn't want
you to marry her. I thought she was cheap—not good
enough for you. And I thought her frightening in a way.
A suggestion of ruthlessness. Plus that look of petulance
and discontent. Plus the way she looked at any man."

"Now, wait. I . . ."

"I'm not just maligning the de—criticizing Laura without a point, Dil. You asked me to keep an eye on her.
I tried, Dil. I called on her twice. The first visit was pretty
cool. The second time I went she wouldn't let me in. I
could smell cigar smoke. She told me she was fine and
there was no need checking up on her. I wondered who
the man might be. I'm a snoop—by profession and, I'm
afraid, by instinct. They came out an hour or so later.
He was a huge blond man, not fat, just terribly big.
They seemed to know each other well. They went to a
restaurant in the Quarter and ate in the patio. Then they
went back to the apartment. I've given his description
to the police. He shouldn't be too hard to find if he's still
in the city. A nosy old lady lives in one of the ground-
floor apartments. She sort of looks after the place. She
lodged a complaint against Laura, charging her with entertaining that man in her apartment at all hours. The
police investigated. There was nothing they could act on."

"I don't believe that."

"Please, Dil. Men have been blind before. It's nothing
against you. And we don't really have any specific evidence against her. It just looks very bad, that's all. We
don't know what her reasons were—or what their re-
lationship was. Laura seemed too self-sufficient to need
any help in anything. Six days ago she phoned me and
said she wanted to see me. Her voice was strange. I
went over there as soon as I could. She questioned me
through the door before she opened it. Anyone could see
that she was terribly frightened—and yet it was a . . . a
calm fright. That doesn't make much sense, does it? She
was frightened in a way that indicated she was used to
being frightened. The draperies were drawn across the
windows.

"I sat down at her invitation and she paced back and

forth in front of me, smoking, her eyes looking out beyond the room. You know the sort of lazy way she talked? She didn't talk that way any more. Sharp and hard and fast, and—older.

"She asked me if I had a place where I could put her up for a few weeks. Privately. She wasn't asking. She was demanding. I said it could probably be arranged. She went and looked down into the street and stood for a long time absolutely still. I don't even think she was breathing. She turned away abruptly. She told me she had changed her mind. She laughed in a very bitter way. I asked her if she was in some sort of trouble. She laughed again and said that you could say the world was in some sort of trouble. I told her I wanted to help her. She went to the door and held it open and thanked me for coming. She thanked me as though she were laughing at me. She said something funny. I can remember the exact words. She said it slowly and carefully, as though she wanted me to remember the exact words. 'My dear, if my bargaining position is not as sound as I hope it is, you can tell Dillon for me that things are not always what they seem to be.' "

"That sounds as though . . ." I said. I didn't want to finish the thought.

"I've been trying to make sense out of it, Dil. She was bargaining with somebody. Her life was at stake. She knew that. She had something to trade for her life, and the trade wasn't good enough. But what?"

"Then you wrote me? I'm glad you did, Jill."

"I was going purely on hunch in writing you. I went down to the street and I wanted to know what she saw out the window. There was a man across the street. Leaning against the side of that building painted pink. I don't know if he was the one. It seemed odd he should stand in the sun when he could have crossed over and waited in the shade, if he were waiting for someone. He was just standing cleaning his fingernails with a broken match. A very ordinary-looking person. A rayon cord suit and a cocoa straw hat with a maroon band and one of those fair, sandy, tight, give-nothing faces. The end of his nose was sunburned. One of those men who can be a car salesman or a tourist from Syracuse or a hired assassin. If it is the third choice, there was something dreadful about him, standing there in the sun—something dreadful and ordinary, like the villain in a Hitchcock film. He looked at me, and it could have been the way any man looks at a girl. I've given his description to Captain Paris, too."

I thought of the man she saw, of the broken match paring grime from ridged nails, of those same hands twisting the wire tight around Laura's throat, the face serious and intent and workmanlike.

I stood up, and Jill's face, her eyes worried, drifted across my eyes and then I was out of the air-conditioning, walking blindly through the heart of New Orleans in July, the drugged, sodden heat that eddies up out of the swamplands and compounds itself by glinting off chrome and rebounding off stone. A man cursed me as I shouldered him aside. When some of the blindness went away I found myself walking down Canal toward the river. I crossed over and turned down Burgundy and went into a dim bar that was like a dark cave amid sun-blasted rocks. The bartender set my drink in front of me. As my eyes adjusted I saw a sallow girl fiddling with a piano so small it was like a child's toy. She had a constant dry cough. A tremendous buff-colored cat sat in regal pose on the corner of the bar. It stared at me with leonine contempt.

The drinks slid down my throat into nothingness. I was nothing. I saw the image of nothing in the blue mirror behind the ranked bottles. Nothing with cropped black hair and blunt features and Indian cheekbones and a level mouth and a look of violence.

The bar did not exist, and the semblance of reality was but projected imagination. I proved it by passing my hand through the buff-colored cat. But my hand touched fur and the writhe of quick muscles and my hand came back with three reddening lines across the back while the bartender laughed deep in his throat.

When I went out it was dusk and the sidewalk was domed, like one half of a concrete pipe. I could walk steadily along the ridge of it if I were careful. But when

I stepped carelessly I fell down over the rounded edge either into the side of a building or into the street. Children followed me and I knew they were intent on my efforts to walk the top of the pipe and I tried harder for their sake. The dusk was purple and blue and the shadows on the pipe were tricky. Neon crackled and buzzed and throaty music thumped from the bars.

I slipped again and turned my back as I fell against the building. I stood with my legs braced and my eyes closed, the city going around me in a slow sick wheeling, the ache and wanting for Laura like a barb through my heart.

A hand fumbled against me and I reached down and caught a thin·wrist. The child who had been trying to pick my pocket yanked her hand free and danced away, shouting something I couldn't understand. The child with her mass of tumbled dark ringlets, face like chalk, eyes like velvet, was so beautiful that I wanted to cry.

The car stopped then and Jill came toward me, drifting easily over the steepness of the sidewalk. I wanted to tell her what I had learned about reality, about shadows in all substance and substance in all shadows. That truth is a girl who coughs, or a buff cat, or a child who looks like an angel. There were no words, and then I was in a car. Then I was in a room, being undressed, and when I looked I saw that there was a tall young man with a ludicrously tiny head, as round as a small pumpkin, heavy glasses, bad complexion. I laughed at him and I was still laughing when he turned out the light and closed the door. I laughed alone in the darkness and listened to the sound of laughing until I turned my face into the pillow and knew that it had only seemed to be laughter. Death crouched in the darkness, and it took the form of a buff cat with Laura's sherry eyes.

Chapter Three

Sam Spencer stared heavily at me across his desk. He was a huge man with a white face that hung in folds, ancient muscles billowed in fat.

Sam is legend. Twenty years ago in Texas a cable snapped and a tool string smashed across his hips and thighs. His wife, Betty, sat by the bedside, waiting for a moment of consciousness that would come before death. She knew her husband well, knew the force of him, the monumental stubbornness.

When he stirred and opened his eyes she said sharply, "Sam? The doctor says you're going to die."

Sam closed his eyes. He sighed. She thought she had lost. Then Sam opened one eye. His voice was like a wind blowing gently through a cave. "Tell that doc to tend to his doctorin' and I'll tend to Sam Spencer."

In four months he was sitting up and eating like a horse. He never walked again. He retired five years ago, and when Betty died he came with Trans-Americas, which was glad to have him.

"I'll get you back to work," he said. "I'll work you, boy. I'll work you until it'll take three of you to make a man's shadow."

"No, Sam," I said.

His big chest lifted as he sighed. "What good can you do? I talked to Paris. He's through with you. He doesn't want you around. This is his business, not yours."

"It's my business, Sam."

He pulled his thumb, cracking the knuckle. "Boy, listen. A year ago Dumont asks me who can maybe come along and fill this chair. I tell him you. He says I'm crazy. I tell him you're steadying down. Mean anything?"

"Later it might, Sam. I don't know. Right now it doesn't mean a thing. Thanks, though."

"You gotta be heroic, eh? Go plunging around and make like catching murderers. A movie boy. Amateur cop. Maybe Dumont was right, boy."

"Think about it, Sam. Use your head. Put yourself where I'm standing."

He closed his eyes. He looked like an old white toad, sunning himself. "Engineers!" he said softly. "Better I should be house mother to a sorority. Twenty years ago I could take you out in the hall and beat it out of you."

"Never," I said. "Not with fists. Not with a club."

He opened his eyes. "How are you fixed?"

"Money? I've been banking my pay for five years. Twenty thousand or so I've got. And then Laura's dough. She banked it here the day she arrived. She had cash and bearer bonds she converted to cash. I get that, I guess. Around a quarter of a million. I don't know what taxes will do to it."

He whistled with surprise. "And I was going to give you a bonus to keep you going until you get all this nonsense out of your system. Maybe you won't ever want to go back to work."

"I'm one of those suckers who work for more than the dough involved. I work because it's something I can do and like to do."

"Let me know when you're ready to come back," he said.

I stood up. "How did you find me?"

"Jill phoned. She said they'd found you in the Quarter and bedded you down in a room at the Bayton. She'd feel better if you left town. So would I. So would Paris."

"They're calling Laura things," I said. "I know she wasn't like that. Part of staying is proving she wasn't."

"Get out of my office," he said wearily.

I went to the apartment. The third-floor hallway was empty. The key slid easily into the lock. Eleven in the morning. The door clicked shut behind me. I had the crazy impulse to call her name. I just said it with my lips, without sound.

I couldn't feel much of anything. I had expected to feel a lot. I went to the closet. Her clothes hung there, with the scent of her on them. I crushed the fabrics in my hands.

19

I picked up the left shoe from a pair I didn't remember. The shoe was new, but the sole was peeled open, the heel broken loose. All her shoes were like that. Somebody had looked hard for something. I wondered if he had found it. I wondered what it was.

The bureau drawers had been pretty well messed up. I guessed that they had been dumped out and the police had later put the things back in. The papers I had read over black coffee that morning told how the body had been discovered at three in the morning, an estimated three hours after she died. One of those accidents. The man on the floor below had come home a little stoned. He had gone up two flights instead of one and had walked into what he thought was his own apartment. Except for that accident, I might have walked in on her.

I sat on the edge of the bed and smoked. Funny there was so little reaction. After a time I went into the bathroom. Her yellow toothbrush was in the holder. That did it. The storm didn't last long. After it was over I felt different. Cold and quiet, almost nerveless. I knew that I could go on. Anguish was carefully locked away in a deep and private place. After this was all over maybe I could take it out again. Maybe it would still be fresh and sharp. But I had no more time for it now. Anger and pain had changed to a new emotion. There was enough money, and all the rest of time. The world wasn't going to be big enough for him to hide in. I would find him. It was that simple. I knew that I would find him.

It made me remember a day long ago, and a beefy sadistic kid named Ronny who was three years older than my eleven. It was a cold day in the vacant lot with the wind whining around the piles of lumber. The kids stood and watched us through that nightmare fight. I was crying with anger as he kept knocking me down, and after a while the blows didn't hurt any more. It was a kind of floating. An entranced monotony. And suddenly I knew, with perfect confidence, that I could not lose. Those who watched us no longer yelled. They stood with sick faces. When at last he went down, he stayed down. They pulled me off him. I spent a week in bed. A small scar at the corner of my mouth is all that remains. And once again I felt that same unfounded confidence.

If the coldness had not come over me, I could not have forced myself to stay in the apartment. Now I could. The many evidences of Laura no longer had the power to sicken me. I packed her clothes in her expensive initialed luggage, crisscrossed with fresh knife slits, and stacked them in the back of the closet. There was an empty carton under the sink. I filled it with jars and tubes and bottles of cosmetics and set it out in the hall. I took the yellow-handled toothbrush out and tossed it on top of the carton.

I hung my own clothes in the closet. I left the door open because the inside of the closet was strong with the scent she liked best.

The ringing of the phone startled me. I hadn't realized that a phone had been installed. It took long moments to find it on the broad window sill behind a drapery.

"This is Zeck. Hoped I'd find you there. We're releasing the body. Any special place you want?"

"Wherever you say, Lieutenant."

"Halbert and Rune, then. They're in the book. You phone and tell 'em. They'll know what to do. Inquest is this afternoon. Pick you up at two?"

I agreed. I phoned Halbert and Rune and made the arrangements. The man asked about her rings. I told him to bury them with her. I told him the denomination and he said he'd get somebody for a short service.

The formal proceedings at the inquest were quick and emotionless. "By hand of person or persons unknown." I was sworn in and asked a few simple questions. How had I been advised to return from Mexico? Did I know of any new friends she might have made? Was there no mention of anything in a letter that might help? Jill was kept a bit longer and questioned closely about her final interview with the deceased.

Jill and Tram went with me to the funeral chapel and then to the cemetery the following morning at ten. The cemetery was out on Gentilly Road. The plot was tiny and expensive. They do not dig deep graves in New Orleans. They dig down about eighteen inches and put in a concrete slab. The coffin rests on that, encircled by cement blocks. Later workmen roof over the block enclosure, cover the whole rectangle with smooth cement, and paint it white. The marble with the inscription is set into the end. The whole thing can be of marble slabs if you want it that way.

It was like I wanted it. Just her name—Laura Rentane Bryant—and the dates. It was most odd to stand there and hear the murmur of the voice of burial mingling with the thrusting roar of traffic on Gentilly. I put a spray of yellow orchids on top of the coffin. Yellow orchids for Laura. And yet, who was Laura? I had to find out. Laura was a girl I had married. She was only a portion of this woman we had just buried.

Tram Widdmar, a bellowing man with the general look of a vast cupid about to tell a questionable story, was as subdued as I have ever seen him. After it was over I wanted to walk, and I asked Jill to walk with me. We walked slowly west on Gentilly. We stopped in a supermarket and bought a loaf of bread and took it into a small park. We sat on shaded grass and flipped bread balls out to the ducks and swans.

"What next, Dil?" she asked at last.

"Find a loose end somewhere and catch hold and hang on until something comes loose."

"And if there are no loose ends?"

"There will be. Somewhere."

"Paris got word from Washington. No passport issued in that name. She had a passport. Bill French saw it."

"I saw it too," I said. "I kidded her about the picture. That's when she promised she'd have a new one taken. It's gone."

"Maybe that was what the killer searched for in the apartment, Dil."

"No. He looked in places too small to hold a passport."

"I'm assigned to the case, Dil. It's good newspaper stuff. Mystery killing of lovely woman. They want me to keep it alive as long as I can. If you find that loose end you spoke about . . ."

"I'll tell you. Unless by telling you I spoil my chances."
She looked out across the pond. "Why should I feel so afraid, Dil?" she asked in a small voice. "Why should I feel so afraid?"

Chapter Four

IT WAS easy to tell Jill Townsend that I was going to find a loose end and hang on. It made me sound like a big operator. I was dramatizing myself. You do things like that. In a sense Jill was the girl with the hair ribbon watching me hang by my knees from the apple tree.

Maybe I was kidding myself about getting hold of a loose end. I wasn't kidding myself about the anger. That was with me. That was something I could taste.

We fed the ducks and then walked back to where Jill had left her little car parked near the cemetery entrance. One day maybe I'd be able to go back in there and look at her grave. Not yet. Not for a long time.

Jill dropped me off on the far side of Canal from the corner of Bourbon and she went on back to her newsroom. I walked down the shady side of Bourbon, trying to forget all the emotions twisting around inside me, trying to think it out as logically as I could. So far there were three unknown factors. One, the huge blond man; two, the tight-faced sandy guy with the sunburned nose; three, Laura's enigmatic statement about things not being what they seem to be.

At least there was one point of contact with the big blond man—the old doll who had lodged the complaint. I remembered her from the time when Laura had rented the apartment. I hadn't liked her then. Now I was more certain than ever that I didn't like her.

I stopped in at a small bar and grill and ate a greasy hamburger. I walked to the apartment. The people on the street were suffering with the heat. Two female tourists, obviously northern schoolteachers, walked by me trying to keep up a holiday spirit. But their dresses were pasted to them and the heat had turned their faces to putty gray. One creature came mincing down the sidewalk toward me as I turned in at the sidewalk doorway to the apartment. It wore a pale blue linen suit, a man's suit, a Panama hat. It wore a blue veil and a necklace of coral beads. The heat didn't seem to bother it a bit. It smirked at me through the veil.

A dime-store cardboard sign was fastened to the old lady's ground-floor apartment door with gilt thumbtacks. I pressed the bell and heard the distant dingle of the inside bell. The door opened so suddenly that it surprised me. I hadn't heard her approaching. The apartment behind her was dark as night. She blinked out at me. She had a small blotched squirrel-like face, surrounded by tangled masses of gray hair. Even in all that heat she was wearing a shapeless cardigan sweater over a cotton dress so faded you couldn't tell what the original print was. I saw why she had been so soundless. Her crumpled old feet were bare.

"I know you," she said. "You're her husband, ain't you?"

"Yes. I want to talk to you."

"I got nothing to say to you, Mr. Bryant. A while back, of course, before she got herself killed, I would have had a lot to say to you about her carrying on and all, but now there isn't anything to say."

She started to shut the door. I stuck my foot in and I guess she forgot she was barefooted. She took a healthy kick at my shin, then gave out a little yelp and started hobbling around in a circle, moaning. I went in and shut the door. It was so dark I could just make her out.

"I'll have the law on you! Forcin' yourself in here on a . . ."

"Look, I live here. Maybe I just want to complain about the decorating."

She went over and sat down and started rubbing her bruised toes. "You want to ask questions about her, don't you? Well, I'm not getting mixed up in it."

I leaned against the door and lit a cigarette. It was self-protection. The apartment smelled rancid, old, weary.

"Did you ever stop to think that maybe you *are* mixed up in it?"

She was utterly still for several moments. "How do you mean that?"

"Suppose they pick up the big blond man, the one she was entertaining and the one you complained about. Suppose he killed her. Who else is going to be the police witness that he used to come to see her? Maybe the big man will have friends who won't want you to live long enough to testify."

I could almost hear the wheels turning over in her mind.

"I didn't see nobody," she said with sullen emphasis.

"Oh, come now! It's all on the police blotter."

"You're just trying to scare me," she said, and there was the hint of a moan behind the words.

"You know enough to be able to scare yourself. Maybe you'd like somebody on your side. I want to know who killed my wife. I want to know about the big blond man who came to see her."

"I don't know anything," she whispered.

I opened the door. "O.K.," I said casually. "Suit yourself."

As I got one foot out into the hallway she said, "Don't go away, Mr. Bryant."

I shut the door again. "Tell me about him. Maybe I can find him. Maybe it's safer for you if I find him instead of the police."

She sat huddled in the dark room, unmoving. When she spoke it was in a dim, faraway voice, as though she were thinking aloud. "A big man, a great big man. Not really fat. The weather bothered him. You could see that. Always sweating. He'd go up the stairs at all hours and the whole place would creak. I don't like stuff like that going on. I get the apartment free because I look out for the place. I could lose my job."

"How did he dress?"

"Always white suits and no necktie. Dark shirts."

"Deep voice?"

"I only heard him talk once. A little thin high voice

25

he has. With an accent. I don't know what kind. That hair of his, blond and worn real bushy in back."

I couldn't get any more out of her. When I walked out into the relative brightness of the hallway it was like coming out of a movie. There was that same moment of directional hesitation. I went up to the apartment. The box of cosmetics was gone. The scent of Laura was still in the place. I opened the French doors onto the narrow balcony with its eroded crust of lacy wrought iron and looked down into Rampart Street two stories below. Laura had looked down into the street and decided against asking Jill to help her. Laura had walked down that same street with a big blond man with a high voice, a man who sweated a lot in the heat.

I phoned the *Star News* and asked for Jill. As I waited I could hear the busy clacking of the wire-service machines. She came on the line with a crisp, businesslike note in her voice. I could see how she would look there, gray eyes scanning the interrupted copy, face wryly out of line, yellow pencil in her dark hair, possibly a carbon smudge on her cheek.

"This is Dil," I said.

Her voice dropped a full scale. "I'm so glad you called. I was worried about you, Dil. You acted so strange when I dropped you off. I'll be through here in . . ."

I interrupted her. "Look, you told me that Laura and the big guy went to a restaurant and ate out in the courtyard. What place was it?"

"The Court of Three Flags, Dil. Over on . . ."

"I know the place."

"Dil!"

"What is it?"

"You're not thinking clearly about this. You can't. It's three o'clock now. Tram asked me to come out for a drink at his place before dinner. I'll pick you up."

"I'm no good for a party now, Jill. Besides . . ."

"I know. You met Laura at Tram's house. It won't hurt you to go back out there. They send pilots right back up. I'll be in front of your place at five-fifteen." She hung up on me.

I went to the Court of Three Flags. To enter the res-

taurant you turn through an arched doorway and walk
along a dark, scabrous hallway lined with peeling murals
of New Orleans history. At the end of the hallway is a
bar facing a huge fireplace. Beyond the bar is the open
courtyard with fish and fountains and greenery and
starched waiters. It's one of those places that's half tourist trap, half legitimate eating place. At that hour of the
afternoon the late lunchers had departed and the early
evening crowd hadn't arrived. There was a drugged sleep-
iness about the place. A bartender polished a glass endlessly, his eyes half closed.

I climbed onto a perilously high bar stool and he
shuffled over to me. Grief is a funny and unexpected sort
of thing. Instead of saying, "Good afternoon," I wanted to
say, "I buried my wife today." It was right on the tip of
my tongue before I got myself under control again.

I ordered Scotch on the rocks and he built it in an
Old-Fashioned glass and put it in front of me. As he
started to wander away, I said, "I'm trying to find out
something. A couple of weeks ago a tall woman with plat-
inum-blonde hair came in here and had dinner in the court
out there with a huge guy in a white suit, a guy with blond
hair worn long in back, a high voice, and an accent."

He turned toward me and opened his eyes wide for the
first time. Black, alert eyes, like the eyes of a wary
animal. His face was the shape of an inverted pyramid,
wide across the forehead, slanting down to a pointed,
rather feral chin. He had dusty black hair and lips so red
they looked bloody.

"What are you trying to find out?"

I hunched forward a little. I winked at him. "The lady
was my wife, friend. I'm trying to find out who she was
with. I want to find out who waited on them."

He shrugged. It was very Gallic. "All kinds we get. Big,
little, fat, thin. A million blondes. We do a big business.
You tell me what time of day and what table, maybe I can
tell you the waiter."

"Maybe I can find out and tell you tomorrow."

He shrugged again. "It won't do no good, mister. What
does a waiter know?"

"He'd know if the man is a regular customer."

27

The bartender closed his eyes for a moment. "Big blond guy with hair long in back, and a high voice?"

"That's right," I said eagerly.

"There's one guy like that I see a few times. I haven't seen him lately. About six-four, maybe two hundred seventy pounds. Shoulders like an ox."

"Do you remember anything else about him?"

"Wait a minute now. Don't rush me. Something about a drink order. Me, I remember the drink orders."

He turned and stared at the bottles on the back bar for inspiration. He snapped his fingers. "Now I got it! Straight gin, imported, no ice, in a cocktail glass with a couple drops of orange bitters. Of course, it could still be the wrong guy."

"It isn't," I said. My voice was a croak. I remembered the little bottle of orange bitters, half used, that I had found in the apartment kitchen, and the three quarts of House of Lords gin.

I finished my drink, paid for it with a five-dollar bill, and waved away the change. As I started away he said, "It isn't none of my business, Mac."

"What isn't?"

"That guy. I remember him a little better now. If you want to make trouble, you better go after him with one hell of a big club. Don't let the voice and the hair fool you. In this business you get so you can pick the fakes. That boy is rough. He's got a real cold blue eye."

I turned back to the bar and wrote down my phone number. I gave him another ten. "If he comes in, you phone me. Keep phoning me there until you get me."

"Who do I ask for?"

"Mr. Bryant."

He stood very still for a long moment and then pushed the ten back across the bar. He looked sad, as though he were disappointed in me. I knew then that the name was a mistake.

"What's the matter?" I asked him.

"I read the papers, friend. I even remember names. No, thanks. No part of this for me."

He went back to polishing his glassware. His eyes were half shut again. He didn't hear anything I said.

In five years Tram Widdmar had built the sagging firm he inherited into one of the strongest import-export outfits in the city. To do so, he had had to make a clean break with the traditional methods of doing business. Maybe it was as a symbol of the break that he had hired the Brazilian architect to design his new home, and had sold the ancient Widdmar home to a historical society.

The new place is built of glass and stone and cypress. It doesn't look out upon anything. It looks inward, at its own enclosed court, and somehow gives the impression not of cold, objective function, but of warmth and pleasure and good living.

There were a few other cars there when we arrived, including one Cisitalia the color of a bluebottle fly, and one Jaguar in battleship gray.

Tram was holding court in a shady corner of the huge patio. He wore a faded sarong tied around his thick brown waist. The group turned and looked at us as we walked diagonally across the patio. It was so close to being the same group as on the afternoon I had met Laura that it gave me a feeling of unreality. The rest of them knew it too, and I could feel the constraint in the air before Tram broke it with his booming welcome. Even Jill was dressed much as she had been on that day—a lacy Mexican half blouse pulled down off her slim shoulders, her midriff bare above the hand-blocked Mexican skirt. It seemed in that moment that I would once again look beyond Tram and see Laura standing there, see the speculative interest in her sherry-brown eyes, that once again our eyes would meet and cling for a moment and everything in the world would be changed for us.

Even Bill French, who had brought her to Tram's cocktail party, was there. He has a lean clever face with a gathering of weather wrinkles at the corners of his outdoor eyes. I mumbled greetings to all those I knew and acknowledged the introductions to those I didn't.

Sammy, Tram's Negro butler, was tending the bar. "The usual, Mr. Brvant?" he asked, reaching for the Scotch.

I did a childish thing. I made my voice a bit too loud and said, "Just straight gin with a dash of orange bitters, Sammy. No ice." I looked around at the faces of all those people I had always considered to be my friends, blackly suspicious of every one of them. I don't know what sort of reaction I expected. My manner must have been very strange. Probably they were just startled. But they looked like strangers—like people I had never seen before. In that moment I wondered if they were all in some vast and evil conspiracy.

Jill took my arm and said, "Goodness, what a revolting-sounding drink, Dil!"

They all laughed, a bit too loudly, and Sammy made the drink with a pained expression and handed it to me. More guests arrived as I drank it. The warm gin was nauseous, but I choked it down. It hit my stomach and seemed to explode in all directions.

After the second one, things got a bit vague. I found myself over by the pool, sitting on the edge of it in the dusk shadows with Bill French beside me. He had been talking and I couldn't remember what he was talking about. I frowned and concentrated on what he was saying.

". . . sure was quite a hunk of woman, Dil. God, on the way north she used to take sun baths every day. Right out on the boat deck. Had a white terry-cloth outfit. A pair of tight trunks and a narrow little halter. The old *Mobile* never had the brightwork polished so much as on that trip. The crew went around glassy-eyed."

"Was she friendly?"

"Hell, no. Couldn't get a word or a smile out of her until the last day out. You could have knocked me over with a pinfeather when she came up to me and started to be chummy. That's when I asked her to go to the anniversary party. She asked about hotels and I recommended the Bayton."

I knew that I had been stupid in not thinking of Bill French before. What I was doing was trying to reconstruct a dead woman. I had to find out about her. Once I learned all about her, I would know who had killed her, because then I would know why she had been killed. I fought back the liquor mists from my brain.

"I supposed you noticed her when she came aboard at Buenos Aires, Bill."

30

"Sure did," he said feelingly. "You know how you wonder about passengers. You could see she had connections, the way she got handled at the dock. A big blond guy took her right through all the red-tape artists as though they weren't there. Hey!"

I realized that I had grabbed hold of his arm. "An enormous blond man, Bill?"

"Yeah. I was at the head of the gangplank, and he asked me where Miss Rentane's cabin was. With his hair long that way and his high voice, you could figure him for some sort of a pansy. But not when he looked right at you. He had an accent. I'd say Dutch or German. He acted like a big shot."

"Bill, how did Laura act on the trip? Did she seem nervous or anything?"

"Not a bit. One thing, though. We made all the usual stops. Rio, Trinidad, Havana. She never got off the ship. She stayed right in her cabin. No, I wouldn't say she seemed nervous. More like she was . . . disinterested."

"How about when you docked here?"

"I don't know about that. I'm pretty busy usually. We were rushing to get through for the celebration, you know. I told her when I'd pick her up at the Bayton."

There was no more information he could give me. Some of the guests had left. Jill asked me if I was ready to go. I thanked Tram and said good-by and we went out to Jill's car and rode back into town. I took her to dinner and put a steak down on top of the tepid gin.

"Are you getting anywhere, Dil?" she asked me, her gray eyes intent.

"Me? Not getting a thing, honey."

"Dil, you're an engineer. What happens when the governor breaks on a machine?"

I shrugged. "Maybe it revs up to where it shakes itself to pieces."

"Don't shake yourself to pieces, Dil. Let Captain Paris and his people handle it. Leave it to men like Barney Zeck. This is their affair."

I looked at her. "And mine. And thanks, Jill, for talking about engineering. You know what we do? We dig a hole and stuff dynamite in it. Then we rig a bunch of geo-

31

phones at intervals. We run the leads from the geophones back to the electronic stuff in the shed. Then we blow the dynamite. The geophones pick up the echoes of the explosion bouncing off the substrata. We get a map of what's underground. And that's what I need to know about Laura. The substrata. I've got to plant some geophones around and then arrange an explosion."

She reached out and caught the first two fingers of my right hand in her fist. "Dil, listen to me. Do you *want* to know what she was? Maybe she was something—unclean. Maybe it won't be good to know."

"Don't talk to me like that," I said. She took her hand back quickly and I thought I saw the glint of tears standing in her eyes before she turned her head away quickly. Then she smiled and was casual and we said good night by her car and I watched her drive away, moving too fast for the traffic.

Chapter Five

AN HOUR after I said good night to Jill, I found myself on Royal Street standing in front of a place called the Rickrack. The Quarter comes alive at night. Walking down Bourbon or Burgundy or Royal is like standing on the curb while a parade goes by. As one band fades, the next one comes thumping along. As you pass each joint a wave of sound comes out of it with almost enough force to knock you down. The doormen in garish uniforms yelp at you to step right in, the show's about to begin. B-girls with bad teeth give you the sloe eye. Strippers inside the joints work out routines using balloons, feathers, parrots, lovebirds, snakeskins. In the hot weather they sweat as they work, and it streaks their powder and makes their bodies glisten.

Sailors and whores, drunken brokers and glassy-eyed schoolmarms, B-girls and pimps and college kids and ragged children and Air Force enlisted men drift up and down the sidewalks looking for something that is never there and never will be there. They are the forthright and honest ones. There are the others who infest the Quarter and come out into the lights after dark. Those with the dark and twisted minds, perpetually sneering at all evidences of a lusty normalcy.

I had pushed through the crowds, and slowly the feeling had come over me that I was being followed. I stopped from time to time and leaned against building walls and waited. I could not pick any specific person out of the crowd. Yet each time I turned and continued on my way there was a prickling feeling at the back of my neck. Once I spun around quickly. Some teen-age girls, arms linked together, laughed at me. I felt like a fool. But still the impression persisted. It was as though the person who followed me could anticipate my movements, could melt into a doorway the moment I began to turn around.

It was then that I saw the poster outside the Rickrack. Papa Joliet on the piano. Papa Joliet with the Uncle Tom fringe of white hair, the long, sad, unmoving face, the lean dancing black fingers. Old Papa from 'way, 'way back. There's one phonograph record worth forty dollars a copy. I own one copy, in storage. It's a little ditty called "Ride on Over." A pickup group. Satch on the horn, the Kid on the tram, Baby on the drums, of course, and Papa Joliet playing that piano.

I went in and the place was dim. Conversation was a low rumble. The piano was on a small platform in the far corner, a small spot wired to the ceiling so that it slanted down on the keys. I went through to a table in the back, near the piano, and sat down with my back to the wall. Around me were other tables of people who had come in to hear Papa. They glared up toward the bar, toward the noisy ones. I remembered how I had brought Laura to hear Papa Joliet and how she had got nothing out of it, though she pretended to.

It was dark back against the wall. I shut my eyes and listened to the piano. It didn't take long to understand what Papa was doing. He was amusing himself by imitating other pianists. The hard Chicago drive of Albert

33

Ammons. The bursting originality of Tatum. The dead-sure beat of Fatha Hines. The gutty strut of Fats. He did imitations with good humor, with subtle exaggeration.

I felt someone close beside me and I gave a grunt of surprise as I opened my eyes. There had been two empty chairs at my table. Now a girl was in one of them. She had her elbows on the table, her chin on her palms. Papa's spotlight made a reflected luminescence against her face.

I decided that, for a B-girl, she was very, very nice. A special one. Heavy thrusting cheekbones, dark blonde hair, a Slavic tilt to her eyes, a wide, rather heavy mouth, and a look of utter repose. She wore a pale dress, strapless, and I could not tell the color because of the dimness. It was cut so low that the cleft between her large firm breasts was a dark pocketed shadow.

"You don't mind?" she said in a startlingly deep voice. Almost a man's voice, and yet intensely feminine.

"I don't mind. But don't be too greedy. I'll pay brandy prices for iced tea if you don't drink too much tea."

The music lovers around us glared at us. Somebody shushed us. She moved her chair around until her bare shoulder brushed my sleeve. Her scent was jasmine and it was heavy. There was a big purse in her lap.

She laughed softly up at me, her breath warm against my face. "Oh, no! I buy my own drinks. It is just awkward to come here alone to hear the music. Men misunderstand. I just hoped you would not mind." She whispered so softly that no one around us was annoyed.

"I don't mind. Stick around," I said. I leaned my head back against the wall and shut my eyes. I wanted to shut her out of my mind, but I could not. She was so close I could feel the warmth of her body, and the jasmine scent surrounded us.

Papa finished a number. "He is so good," she said softly.

"The best," I said.

Papa started a noisy one. "Glendale Glide." I looked down into my new friend's face. I took a healthy pull at my drink. She rubbed her cheek against my sleeve.

"You think I am crazy," she said softly. "This is such a crazy thing to ask. But I have listened to this music with someone I love who is now no longer here. If you would put your arm around me, I could pretend so much easier. It is dark here. No one will mind. And that is all I want. Just your arm."

"Just my arm," I said. I put my arm around her. She made a motion a kitten will make, snuggling against me. Her dark blonde hair tickled my cheek. She reached an arm across me. She was on my right. She reached an arm over to my left side and I started with the sudden pain as the sharp point dug into my flesh.

"Do not move. Do not cry out," she said huskily. "I don't want to kill you."

"What goes on?"

"Don't move, Mr. Bryant. Enjoy the music. Relax and enjoy the music. Pretend we are lovers."

I started to tense to thrust her away and the point dug deeper. "No," she said softly, "I can feel your muscles tighten. Make them loose again. Ah, better, Mr. Bryant."

As she held the knife in her right hand, out of sight under the edge of the table, her left hand began to creep into my pockets. I looked cautiously over at the nearest table. The two couples there were absorbed in the music. No help there. I felt ridiculously helpless. Her left hand touched my right hip pocket.

"Now move forward just a little bit, Mr. Bryant."

I did so. It took enough pressure off the pocket so that I felt her slip my wallet out. Anybody looking toward us would have seen only a man with his arm around a lush and obviously friendly girl.

I slowly pulled my feet back to get them under me. "Put your feet out where they were," she ordered. "I am not playing a game, Mr. Bryant. This is a long knife. The point is just below your ribs, slanting upward. If I thrust, it will reach your heart."

"Who taught you this?"

"Be still, please. Now reach very slowly into your left trouser pocket and take everything out and place it on the edge of the table."

One thing I was absolutely certain of. She wasn't joking. She knew my name. She was as serious as death itself. And I had no way of defending myself. Any attempt to use my right arm, and she would feel the preliminary tensing of the muscles. I was filled with a helpless anger.

I had my hand in my left pocket when the man came out of the darkness and reached for her. I heard her gasp as he reached and beyond him somebody stood up and swung at the ceiling spot. It popped loudly and Papa's piano faltered into silence. The girl twisted away, out of my arm. I grabbed for her, caught fabric, and felt it tear away. A chair fell over. A woman screamed twice and the room was full of panic. Everybody decided at the same moment to get out of there. I came around the table and somebody grabbed my wrists, strongly. I twisted away and struck at a figure silhouetted vaguely against the lights of the street. It was a good and satisfying blow, and it made that splatting sound that comes only when you strike flesh. Somebody grabbed me from behind. I kicked back hard and somebody grunted as my heel dug into a shin bone.

Then there was a misty movement in front of me. I tried to duck. Half my head fell in on itself like a dynamited chimney and I went down onto both knees, not quite out, but unable to lift my arms. Lights came on. A man yanked me to my feet and I staggered over against the wall, bracing myself. My vision cleared and I saw he was young and well dressed. He looked like a desk clerk in a good Manhattan hotel. The other one was a bit older and heavier. They both looked almost too angry to speak.

The bright ceiling lights were all on, destroying the atmosphere of the place. Papa Joliet sat looking sadly out at the nearly empty room. He shook his head.

"What is this?" I demanded thickly.

The heavier one picked my wallet off the floor and glanced casually into it. I saw the packet of money. He handed it back to me.

"Come on, Bryant. Let's go."

"Let's go where? I'm not going to . . ."

The younger one gave me a look of complete disgust. "Then don't come and don't learn anything," he said.

The flesh was split over his cheek. His eye was rapidly puffing shut.

I followed them out meekly. We walked two fast blocks. The heavier one was limping a bit. I guessed it was from the kick I had landed.

- Their car was a black cheap sedan. The heavier one drove. I sat in the back alone. They turned right on Canal. The young one unhooked a hand mike from a dash bracket, cupped his hand around it, and murmured so low that I could not hear what he said. I realized that it didn't surprise me. From the moment I had decided to accompany them it had been because I had assumed they were police. Something in their manner had been unmistakable.

They turned right on Broad Avenue and went on out to a drive-in on Route 11 and parked where there were no other cars. The trim little carhop came out.

"Better have coffee, Bryant," the younger one said. I was beyond objecting. My head had started to ache from the force of the blow.

"What did you hit me with?" I asked.

"A sap." The coffee came. They passed my cup back to me. It was almost too hot to sip.

The young one turned and looked back at me. "We're sore, Bryant, because something blew up in our face. It was a chance we won't get again."

"Who are you?"

"Just call us the Jones boys. Your record has been checked, Bryant. Just lately it's been triple-checked. Unless you're a hell of a lot cleverer than we think you are, you're clean."

"Gosh, thanks," I said.

"Don't waste your time trying to be snotty with us, Bryant. You pulled a damn fool trick marrying that woman. You . . ."

"That's a line I'm getting damn tired of," I said. "Everybody seems to have decided Laura was a tramp. Where do you people get to know so much?"

"We haven't called her a tramp. And I don't think we will, Bryant. But we'll call her something else. Do you want to know what she was?"

37

"She was my wife."

"Before that, fella. 'Way before that. I'd like to tell
you. I've got permission to tell you, but it has got to
stay under your hat. I want your promise not to spill
any of it to the Townsend girl. This isn't something for
the papers."

I thought it over. I said, "If you tell me something I
didn't know, you've got my promise."

"Now listen good, Bryant, because I'm going to give
it to you fast, and I'm not going to repeat it or attempt
to justify it. Just realize that I'm not saying anything that
hasn't been cross-checked and proved. It's all in her dossier in Washington."

"You make her sound pretty important."

"She was. Her right name was Tilda Renner. During
the war she was the mistress of Ernst Haussmann, one
of the bully boys of the Gestapo."

"Now, look here, I won't . . ."

"Shut up, Bryant. Haussmann was picked up for the
War Crimes Commission. He escaped, most probably with
Tilda's help. Warrants have been out for both of them
since '46. Finally we got them tagged as to location. Haussmann in Spain, where we couldn't grab him,
and the Renner woman in the Eastern Zone of Germany,
where we couldn't reach through the iron curtain and
grab her. We put an agent on her and got back word
she was living with a Red officer, a Colonel General
V. Glinka, doing organization work for the East German
police force, as they call it.

"Then last year we get a rumor that Haussmann and
the Renner woman have gone from Spain to South America. We do some more checking. Our people can't locate
the Renner woman or Glinka. Then Glinka turns up a suicide in Moscow, published in *Pravda* as heart failure.

"The file stays open, but no information. A month ago
a middleman got in touch with the Department of Justice. All he knows is that the Renner woman is in the
United States. She wants to make a deal. She wants amnesty for herself and for Haussmann. In return, she will
turn over a document of 'vital importance.' The funny
thing is, it could be of vital importance. Intelligence

files show that in the middle twenties one V. Glinka helped organize the Russki intelligence net all over the world. He was one of the few big Reds who didn't get tangled with the purge trials of the thirties. But the Justice Department gives the middleman the standard answer. Turn over the document and we'll talk about amnesty later. We were put on it immediately."

"This is crazy talk," I said. "Probably there is somebody named Tilda Renner, but that's no reason to suppose that Laura Rentane was Tilda Renner."

"Even when the description Captain Paris sent the State Department matches perfectly? Even when there's no record of a passport issued to a Laura Rentane? Even when we know that she was knifed trying to get out of the Red zone, and we've seen the X-ray plate of the knife tip in her rib? Even when we know a guy answering Haussmann's description put her on the ship in Buenos Aires and later visited her in Rampart Street?

"There are a lot of people working on this. We want Haussmann. We want that document. We want whoever is trying to get hold of the document. There are so many of us down here now we're falling all over each other. We searched you good the other night. You slept like a baby. We know you haven't any document. We've kept a close tail on you, every minute of the day and night. We knew that if somebody took a hack at you, it would show that they didn't recover that document when they killed the Renner woman. That would leave two choices. You or Haussmann. If this document is as hot as we think it might be, then you can be certain that the people who forced Glinka's suicide are hot after it.

"Tonight we bobbled the ball and got thrown for a loss. Andy, here, was the one who guessed that babe might be holding a knife on you while going through your pockets. We didn't figure on her having a confederate who would smash the lights. It was stupid and we'll probably never get another promotion, but it's over now. Did she clean you?"

"No."

"Good. Then you can still be our little stalking horse, Bryant. Unless they get to Haussmann first and get the document off him, they'll have to take another hack at you. If it's as hot as we think it is, they'll have to follow up every last possibility."

I handed the cup back to be put on the tray hooked to the car door. My hand shook. "It's all so—so unbelievable that I—"

His voice softened. "Sure. You were played for a sucker. But so was Colonel General Glinka, boy. Give us as good a description as you can of the girl."

I did so.

Then he gave me my orders. "Don't try to shake off any tail you happen to suspect. Just stay in circulation, and keep your mouth shut. If there's trouble, just yell as loud as you can."

"Why did Laura want to marry me?"

"She was a gal who never missed a chance, Bryant. She had you with the ring in your nose. If we'd grabbed her, we'd still have convicted her, but you would have raised hell with so many congressmen that you might have got her out sooner or later. Her big mistake was stealing information from the Russkis to use as trading material. They sent her along to join her pal Glinka."

"Is Haussmann still in the area?" I asked.

"We think so. We hope so."

"Why did they have to kill her? Why?"

"Because the entire document might have been in her mind. She might have memorized it. That's the safest way to carry information."

They left me back at the apartment. I locked the door behind me. I had to be alone to think about what they had told me. I told myself that it was a case of mistaken identity. A ridiculous mistake. I tried to laugh at the mistake they had made. The sound came out like a sob. There are some things you have to believe. And I found that I knew, deep inside me, that Laura Rentane was Tilda Renner, had been Tilda Renner.

The parts of the jigsaw puzzle that was Laura fitted together too readily. I hunted through my mind for a way to despise her. I wanted to hate her. It was a desire born of weakness. If I could hate her, I could cease mourning for her.

Instead, I found as I sat there alone in the darkness that I was making excuses for her. Probably Haussmann had taken her when she was too ignorant, too inexperienced, to know what he was. By the time she found out, maybe it was too late. She had then, like a frightened animal, done what she could to save her own life and her own freedom. It had taken a certain courage to do what she had done. Yes, it must have taken a great deal of courage.

And then, frightened and alone, she had come to this country to barter for her freedom. Probably Haussmann, through threatening to kill her, had acquired her cooperation in the barter.

I sat and tried to think of her as evil, and I could not. I thought, instead, of the way her sleeping face had looked on the pillow beside me. I thought of how I had awakened one sultry afternoon and seen her standing silhouetted against the lowering sun, her firm body the color of tea with cream except for the two startling white slashes where the sun suit had protected her body from the sun. I remembered how passion would blind her eyes, and she would speak small, limping, broken words of love.

I remembered the catlike way she cared for her body, how she would call to me and I would go into the thick steamy air of the bathroom and she would hold her silver-blonde hair out of the way with both hands while I scrubbed the long lovely column of her back.

I remembered the days of honeymoon, when night and day are curiously mingled, when there is food at crazy hours. It seemed a memory of perfection, and yet flawed in some obscure way. It took me a long time to isolate and examine the flaw. Even then I was not certain that it *was* a flaw. She had told me often that she loved me, but now I had a certain bitter speculation. Had it been love for me as a person, as a man and an individual, or had it been merely love for me as the faceless, nameless instrument of her gratification? In her, passion had run endlessly strong, endlessly demanding. Now, for the first time, I began to wonder if her strong desires had not been always turned inward to the point where, during

41

the instants of her completion, I was a nameless, voiceless, faceless entity that was good only because it was male.

I went to bed exhausted at three o'clock. It was purely emotional exhaustion. It hadn't come from the girl who had held the knife. Nor had it come from the truths the men in the car had spoken. It came, instead, from some process of growth caused by trying to analyze what Laura and I had had for each other. During those dark hours of thought I became more of an adult. And yet my ultimate conclusion was so pitifully meager that it was like the mountain laboring to produce the mouse.

My conclusion was this: Laura and I had wanted each other, almost from the moment we met. We had been extraordinarily well mated physically. The endless wanting had resulted in something almost hypnotic. Yet the strength of it did not make it good, or even valid. It was far too much on the physical level. I could look back and see that though she was shrewd, clever, alert, she actually had little intellectual resource. She had read nothing. She could not talk abstractly. She ate and slept and cared for her body. Thus it could not be called love, in my understanding of the word, because love must also exist on an intellectual and a spiritual level, as well as emotional and physical.

It took me long hours to decide that perhaps I had not loved her after all. I could not as successfully dramatize my personal position with that new knowledge in mind, and that made the conclusion more difficult. It had been a desperately strong case of physical infatuation.

My conclusion did not in any way lessen my desire to get my hands on the person who had twisted the wire tightly around her throat. In fact, in a most odd way, it strengthened and reinforced my desire, because it made her more vulnerable.

I slid through a wet darkness into nightmare. I was on a boat. I had caught Laura on a cruelly barbed hook. She flopped about, nude, on the floor boards of the boat in her death agony while the guide kept saying it was a common type of fish, but inedible.

Chapter Six

I SLEPT until noon and awakened in that drugged state where dreams seem to cling to the fringes of the mind and cannot be dislodged. The dreams give everything a look of unreality, and make all past experience implausible. In that state it seemed incredible to me that I had been married to anyone named Laura, and more incredible that Laura could have been a notorious person named Tilda Renner. It all seemed like something from a very poor movie, the sort of movie where the characters are yanked around on strings in order to heighten melodrama.

It is possible to understand, objectively, that there are Tilda Renners in this world, and Haussmanns and Glinkas. There is a sickness in the world, and such people are the symbols of the disease. Symptomatic. But it is far more difficult to understand such people in relation to your own life. Life is composed of small daily acts, small attitudes, small opinions. Insert the Renners and Haussmanns and Glinkas into your daily affairs, and the result is dangerously close to comedy. High, lusty comedy in the Shakespearean tradition. People who strut and bellow and wear false noses.

Once I saw a Burmese hillside that stank because tanks with bulldozer blades had covered the Jap-made caves from which they had fired on us, and then the rains had come and had washed away the dirt mounds. At first glance, at first full comprehension, it was a complete horror. Then the mind veered away from comprehension and all that was left was the stink, a troublesome nauseous stink about which everyone complained.

So it is with the Renners and the Haussmanns and the Glinkas. You comprehend them for a moment, and comprehension sickens you, and so you think of them only on the basis of their ability to complicate your own life.

I sat on the bed and smoked the first cigarette of the day and tried to brush away the clinging bits of dreams, the same way you paw your face after walking through a narrow place strung with the webs of spiders.

This day was going to be worse than all the others, I knew. The humidity seemed to have gone up to an impossible high. Sweat ran from my throat and down my chest. The pillow and the sheets were sodden.

I went to the French doors and looked up at the sky. It was a pale brassy blue. I could feel the heat of the sun-drenched street against my face.

I showered and shaved and picked the coolest outfit I could find: white sleeveless shirt, rayon cord slacks, sandals. I looked at myself in the mirror and remembered hearing once upon a time that children do not increase their ability to learn in a regular upward curve. The chart resembles stairs. At intervals there will be a sudden upward jump in the ability to learn. And I wondered if maturity for an adult comes the same way. Possibly I imagined it. There seemed to be a new maturity in my face, a lessening of the look of recklessness. Already, the man who had struck Harrigan, who had come flying back to stare down at the face of his dead wife, seemed to be a stranger.

Plans for the day—none. I was a stalking horse. Make like a target and let the Jones boys stalk the stalkers.

I went to the bureau and distributed my belongings in my pockets. The cash situation was still healthy. I would have to get hold of a lawyer and make arrangements about Laura's money. There was plenty of time for that. I picked up the key chain and looked at the small rabbit, remembering the way Laura had said, "You always give a husband a present."

I had told her it was a pretty symbolic present for a bride to give, and we had laughed. A small golden rabbit about three quarters of an inch high, sitting on his haunches, with little red stones for eyes, one ear lopped over, the ring for the key chain fastened to the tip of the upright ear. It was a fatuous-looking little rabbit

—fatuous and at the same time debauched, hung over. It was the sagging ear that seemed to give that impression.

I was halfway down the stairs when I heard my phone ring. I went back up three stairs at a time, fumbled the key into the lock, and got to the phone before it stopped ringing.

"Hello, Dil? This is Betty."

The voice was vaguely familiar. "Betty?" I said.

"Don't be so *dull,* darling," she said. There was annoyance in her voice and something else. Anxiety, maybe. The voice was oddly familiar.

"Oh, Betty! Sorry to have sounded stupid. How are you?"

There was relief in her tone. "I'm anxious to see you, Dil. It's been so long, hasn't it?"

"It certainly has," I said with feeling. I knew the voice. It was the knife-wielding gal from the Rickrack. She must be afraid, I decided, of a tap on the line. "I'm anxious to see you, too," I said, giving it a certain emphasis.

"Look, darling. I'm going to be terribly busy for a while. When do you think you can be free?" That was clear enough. Free meant without escort.

"That's hard to say. The last time I saw you, I think we both decided, Betty, that I wasn't good for you. How do you know that won't be true again?"

"That's something I'll just have to risk, isn't it?"

"Of course, there's a certain amount of risk on my part too," I said, and forced a laugh.

"Well, I guess you're just too uncooperative, Dil. You seem to forget that a girl has some pride. I saw Monroe Wiedman at three o'clock yesterday afternoon and he told me you were in town. I'm sorry I listened." There was a loud clack and the line was dead.

I hung up slowly. She had been trying to tell me something. I'd never heard of anyone named Monroe Wiedman. I looked up the name in the phone book. It wasn't listed. Yet I knew that it was the clue as to where to meet her at three o'clock. I went down to the heated tunnel of the street and found a place to have brunch. Coffee made my mind work better. I bought a city map at a newsstand, slipping it inside a magazine, and went back to the apartment. In Algiers, across the river, I found the intersection of Monroe Street and Wiedman Street. It was a quarter after one. That gave me an hour and forty-five minutes to shake off my friends and get over there. That is, if I wanted to shake off my friends. It made good sense to try to get in touch with them and tell them, or merely go on over and let them trail along.

But behind the girl's gay and casual voice I had detected fear. I wanted to think it a genuine fear. And if she wanted to lead me into ambush, this seemed a pretty awkward way to go about it. I decided on a compromise. I would shake off my friends, but try to do it in such a way that they could not accuse me of doing it on purpose. I shoved the map in my pocket and walked over to Canal. I went into a big department store and bought some shirts. I made no attempt to find out who was tailing me.

I sauntered over near the elevators, and as one was about to close its doors I hurried over and got in. I got off at the third floor, walked to the back of the store, and went down the stairs and out the fire door at the back. I walked through a parking lot to a parallel street and went down two blocks before turning back onto Canal Street. I took the Algiers ferry at the foot of Canal. There was a faint hot breeze on the Mississippi. At ten minutes of three I stood at the corner of Monroe and Wiedman, bundle in hand. Algiers is as complete a refutation of the romance inherent in the name as its African namesake. It is rough and dirty, with narrow potholed streets and bleary store windows.

At a quarter after three, when I was beginning to wonder if I were getting a touch of heat exhaustion, she came up beside me. She was dressed in the same clothes she had worn in the Rickrack. Her dress was crudely pinned under the arm where I had torn it. There were purple patches of exhaustion under her eyes.

"Come quickly," she said.

I walked down a number of side streets with her. She kept her eyes downcast. She walked as though she were unutterably weary.

"In here," she said. It was a coffee shop. Octagonal tile floor, wire-legged tables and chairs, a smell of disinfectant and burned grease. The only other customer was an old man with his head cradled in his arms on the table. He could have been sleeping or dead. She led the way to a table that was around a jog in the wall, out of sight of the front windows. A ceiling fan creaked slowly overhead.

She sat down and shut her eyes for long seconds. I asked if she wanted some iced coffee. She nodded without opening her eyes. The shuffling waitress set the two glasses down on the imitation marble with more force than was necessary.

The girl opened her eyes and looked at me. I had not been able to see the color of her eyes in the Rickrack. They were green, with small flecks of brown in the iris, close to the pupil.

"You did very well," she said. "I had to watch and make certain you weren't followed."

"What is this all about?" I asked.

"I thought it would be so simple. Now I don't know how to say it. I called you because there is no one else. No one to help, and the trouble is your fault."

"*My* fault! Look, I didn't ask you to . . ."

"Please. I have been up all night and I am not thinking clearly or saying things well, Mr. Bryant." She opened her purse, took something out, and handed it to me. I looked at it under the edge of the table. It was a shoemaker's awl with the metal spike cut off to half its length and resharpened to a needle point.

"What's this?"

She sighed. "Mr. Bryant, I had my orders. I was to put my arm around you. We had to use care in following you, because the others were following you. It could be done in any dimly lighted place where you would sit down. If you stood at the bar, I was to go to you there and get you to sit at a table. I was ordered to put my arm around you. That instrument would be in my hand. There is a place right there. . . ." She leaned over and touched the nape of my neck right at the base of my skull. "A small hollow. I was taught about it very carefully and made to practice how it is done. It is very quick and very good. You wouldn't cry out. You would slump

47

as though falling asleep. When my companions saw that, one of them would join us and we would take everything from your body and leave you there."

I stared at her. "Lovely people you run around with!"

"Please. It would have been very easy but somehow I could not do it. I tried to do it my own way. I did not follow orders. That is a very serious thing. It is something we are not permitted to do. When it failed, I knew I was—as dead as they wished you to be. I didn't want to die. So I ran. Now there is no one I can get to help me. Except you. Maybe you can do nothing. I must have a place where I can sleep, where no one knows I am there. After I have slept, maybe I can start to think again, think how to save myself."

"What kind of a stupid joke is this?" I demanded.

She looked at me, her eyes steady. She said softly, "You can go. Please go now. There is no point in your staying."

I put a quarter on the table for the coffee and got up and walked toward the door. I looked back. Her eyes were closed again. She sat slumped in the uncomfortable chair.

I went back. "Suppose I can find you a safe place. What then?"

Her lip curled. "Someday you people will learn that there is no safe place in all the world. The days of safe places have gone by."

"Do you want help, or don't you?"

"Only if you are willing to help, Mr. Bryant."

I got change from the cashier, looked up a number, and shut myself in the airless, breathless phone booth. It took a long time before I heard Sam Spencer's rumble.

"Sam, this is Dil Bryant. I want—"

"You ready to give up gumshoeing and get back on the job, boy?"

"Not yet, Sam. I need help. Look, have you got any visiting big shots staked out in Paul Harrigan's apartment over on Loyola? Expecting any?"

"There's nobody there now, but in about ten days I expect—"

"I'm coming after the keys, Sam. And don't ask me

any questions. Just trust me. Better yet, have your girl seal the keys in an envelope and leave them with the cashier at that drugstore diagonally across the street from you. Have her tell the cashier a Mr. Robinson will pick up the keys. Can you do that right away?"

"Sure, but——"

"Thanks, Sam," I said, and hung up. Paul Harrigan can afford to keep the apartment in town because Trans-Americas uses it for a billet for visiting brass and pays Paul for its use. It's over in the university section, a ground-floor apartment with a private entrance at the rear of an old, ugly house.

Back at the table I wiped my face with paper napkins from the table dispenser. "It's all set. Ready to go?"

She fell asleep in the taxi that took us from the foot of Canal Street to the drugstore and from there to the apartment. I unlocked the door and she went in ahead of me. The apartment had been redecorated since the last time I had been in it. The dark woodwork had been painted white, the walls done in cool greens and blues.

She let me guide her back to one of the two bedrooms. She sat on the edge of the bed and I went around the room, opening windows, drawing draperies. I started the fan and adjusted it. When I looked around she had lain back on the bed.

I spoke to her and she didn't move. I slipped her shoes off and swung her legs up onto the bed. She mumbled something I couldn't understand. I shook her until her eyes opened.

"Wha'?" she said.

"I'll come back around midnight. That'll give you nearly eight hours' sleep. I'm taking the keys. Do you need anything?"

She frowned. Her voice was far away. "Dress. Toothbrush. Comb. Lipstick. And . . ."

I waited and then looked at her again. She was sound asleep, breathing heavily through parted lips. I stood looking down at her in the darkened room. The fan made a soft purring sound. It seems a violation of privacy to look upon a sleeping stranger. In her sleep she rolled over onto her left side, her right leg drawn up, her hands, palms together, under her cheek. It is the classic pose of a sleeping woman. It exaggerates the curve of hip. Something about her weariness and helplessness brought on desire. Her body had a look of strength. I stood and the blood hammered in my ears louder than the sound of the fan. Then I turned and left. My palms were wet and my hands trembled as I locked the door behind me.

Chapter Seven

NEW ORLEANS has its own unique adjustment to the heat of summer, at least in the Quarter, where the buildings stand shoulder to shoulder. The sidewalks are roofed by galleries supported by iron posts near the curbing. These roofed sidewalks are called, locally, banquettes. The galleries provide a place for out-of-doors living for the people on the second floor. They in turn are roofed. The railings are of ornamental iron patterned in the shape of leaves, usually, because leaves have a look of coolness. Vines grow up the second-floor posts, entwining themselves among the iron leaves, providing the illusion of privacy. There is never a water shortage. It is simple enough to wet down the gallery floor and the casual pedestrian had best keep a wary eye cocked upward for the deluge.

After making the purchases for the girl and putting them in the apartment where she still slept, I walked back into the Quarter, into the long shadows of evening. I saw the galleries and reconstructed in memory the front of the Rampart Street apartment on the edge of the Negro section, and knew that with care those galleries that stretched almost to the corner would give me a chance to shake off my attentive friends.

Barney Zeck was sitting on the top stair when I went up to the third floor. The perennial toothpick was in the corner of his mouth. The heat seemed to affect him not at all.

"Having fun?" he asked mildly as I came slowly up the flight.

"Oh, dandy!"

"The town is full of big-time law brass, Bryant."

"So I've noticed. Come on in and have a drink."

He followed me in. I turned on the fans and brought him his drink. He held it up to the light. He looked like a wise and dusty elf.

"Ramifications," he said softly. "That's the word. A thing like this, it has ramifications. But not for us. Not for me. I see it simple. Dead woman. So catch the killer. Standard procedure. This is off the record, Bryant. 'Way off the record. I'm a sucker to trust you, maybe. But I'm browned off enough not to care. The orders came down from on high. Drop it. Forget it. Nice, isn't it?"

I looked at his cold nailhead eyes. There was anger there. "Why?" I asked.

"Apparently this is some kind of an international deal. And we're just locals. We can fumble the ball. So they whistle us over to the side lines."

I took a long pull at my drink. "Are they going after the killer?"

"In their own way. But I think, Bryant, they're more anxious to make a deal with him than they are to clobber him. And I know you want to get your hands on him. I turned over everything I've learned. But I held out one little thing. I saved it for you. I don't like people who kill women. You tell me you'll use your head and stay cool and I'll give you my little nugget."

"I promise, Lieutenant."

"My favorite pigeon is the big blond guy. I've sifted all our stools. He isn't local. But I got a faint line. Triangulation, maybe. This can be a rough town. Somewhere within a two-block radius of the Café Lafitte at the corner of St. Philip and Bourbon, in an apartment I would have found sooner or later if they'd let me stay on it, somebody is putting on shows. For a special type of people. People who like whips. You know what I mean. The big blond guy goes for that. Anyway, he's been

51

to a couple. Now, don't jump to the conclusion the Lafitte is sour. I'm just using that as a reference point. They
have a couple of shows a week. Admission is a hundred
bucks. You'll have to fumble around until you find somebody who can give you a line on it. The next show is tomorrow night, Saturday night."

"The people from out of town are tailing me, Lieutenant."

"You won't get in unless you shake them off."

"Any suggestions?"

He stood up and yawned. "You'll have to figure that
out. I'd use city busses, myself. One suggestion, though.
If you have a drink at the Café Lafitte, stay away from
the specialty of the house. It's a dry Martini with ab-
sinthe. They call it an Obituary. Good name, too."

He closed the door quietly behind him. All the time
I showered and changed, throughout the late dinner at
Galatoire's, I tried to decide how I would handle Zeck's
bit of information, knowing all the time that my mind was
already made up. The sensible thing to do was to make
contact with the Jones boys and give them the data and
let them put a net around the entire area Zeck had mentioned. But the blood-darkened face and horrid bulging
eyes of Laura kept drifting across the back of my mind
and I knew that I wanted a quiet few minutes with Haussmann. All to myself. If she had tried to cross him up by
leaving him out of the trade for amnesty, he would have
killed her. And I knew that in a few moments with him I
could find out.

At eleven o'clock I went into my act. I went out on
the shallow balcony into the night, stripped to the waist.
I stretched and yawned and went back in. Fifteen minutes
later I put the lights out. At eleven-thirty, dressed in the
darkest clothes I had, I slipped out onto the balcony,
stepped over the railing, lowered myself, hung by my
fingertips, and dropped the last few inches onto the gallery
roof. I crouched against the front of the building, invisible
from the street.

"You hear 'at thumpin', honey?" a lazy voice asked directly below me.

"Din' hear no thumpin'," a woman answered.

I kept low and close to the front of the building. The galleries were of different heights, but they all adjoined. There was a party on one. A party so noisy I could have walked across over their heads trying to stamp holes in the gallery roof. The last gallery was dark, and I stretched out flat and looked down at the sidewalk, thirty feet below. I hunched forward until I could look into the galleries, my head upside down. The screen of vines was thick. I moved to the outside corner and slid down the iron post onto the empty gallery. It was a full ten minutes before there was no pedestrian traffic underneath. I slid down the second post to the sidewalk and walked fast to the corner, hurried around it, and flattened myself in a shallow doorway. No hurrying footsteps, no whistle, no siren.

I came out onto Canal on the Basin Street corner, and got a cab that dropped me a block from Harrigan's apartment.

She was still asleep. The fan whirred softly.

I washed the grime off my hands and read an ancient magazine until twelve-thirty. Then I went into the bedroom, reached over her to the head of the bed, and clicked on the bed lamp.

She sat up with a hard intake of breath, her eyes wide, startled, fearful. She let her breath out with a great sigh.

"Sorry I startled you."

"What time is it, please?"

"After midnight. There's the stuff I bought you. I'll wait out in the other room."

As I waited I heard the far-off drone of the shower, and I thought of the many times I had heard the same sound as I waited for Laura. She had bathed so very often. Almost as though there were some dirt she was trying to scrub off that wouldn't come off. Dirt that Tilda Renner had acquired, and Laura Rentane couldn't remove. Ever.

At last the girl came out. She wore the lime and white print dress I had bought for her. She was barefoot, her dark blonde hair pulled tightly back, and wearing no make-up. She seemed younger than I remembered, and oddly shy. I was on the couch. She sat in a rattan chair facing the couch, one leg pulled up under her. She reached

53

over and took my cigarettes and matches from the coffee table.

"I suppose you want me to talk to you now," she said.

"You suppose right. I always talk to people who hold knives on me. And you baffle me. Sometimes your speech is very American. And then it goes quaint all of a sudden. What's your name?"

"My right name. Talya Dvalianova. I shall tell you the story of Talya. A very stupid story." Her voice was an expressionless monotone. "My father was an engineer at a tractor plant in the Urals. I took competitive examinations. At fourteen I was sent to the special school in Leningrad because I am really quite bright. I have never been home since. I learned to hate everything American. Decadent capitalism, built on blood and oppression. I learned that I would gladly give my life if it would hurt your country. I was tested very carefully. The school is very clever. It has your magazines, prints of your movies, everything needed to teach us to pass in this country as one of you. And other skills were taught. I can kill a man, blow a bridge, plant thermite pencils. You see, I was turned into a weapon and told that I could be as valuable to Russia as a regiment of soldiers. I was proud and happy to be a weapon. I was—dedicated. Six months ago, the day after I became twenty-one, I was taken out of the country. I was taken at last to Havana. There, at night, a small fast boat took three of us to a Florida place. It is called, I think, the Ten Thousand Islands. In a city called Naples two of us were picked up by one of our people in a big car. We became tourists. The other one, whose name I never knew, was taken by someone else up to Birmingham, I believe. I was brought here. Here I am Betty Morin. I work in a dress shop. I have my birth certificate. It tells that I was born in Sharon, Pennsylvania. There are many foreign-born there, to account for my Slavic look. I have memorized street maps of Sharon, directory names of persons living near the house where the certificate says I was born."

All I could do was stare at her.

"One thing we were taught, over and over. Do not be taken in by how good life *seems* to be in this country. I was given no assignment. Each week I met the man to whom I report. I asked for work. He told me to be patient. The way it is organized, he is the only one I know. I cannot tell you just how it was. I tried to become Betty Morin, that Betty Morin from Sharon. Maybe I tried too hard. This Betty Morin, she became very contented. She went to movies. She bought pretty dresses from her pay. She had dates. It is hard to stay dedicated when one is having fun. For the first time. To Betty Morin the school at Leningrad became far away. Like something in a dream. This was new. Not to be watched all the time. To be free to come and go. Betty Morin sold pretty frocks. Betty Morin began to wonder if she could leave this city and go to another city or a small town, and continue to be Betty Morin. And last week, when I reported, the man was very excited. He said there was work. Important work. Emergency work."

"Did he explain what it was?"

"He said that an important man had turned traitor and had given highly important data to a woman. He said the important man had been purged, and that the woman had reached New Orleans and wished to give the data to your government. It—it made me forget the dreams of Betty Morin. Once again I was Talya Dvalianova. I had work to do. Last night we followed you."

"Just the two of you?"

"And two others whose faces I did not see. We learned that you were being clumsily followed by two men. You know the rest. I was instructed to kill you. Even two months ago I could have done it easily. Talya could have done it. Betty could not. I have become soft, Dillon Bryant. It is so hard to be two persons. And now, of course, I must be found and killed. I have a dream. I dream that I can go away and be Betty Morin in truth, with nothing left of Talya. But it is only a dream. There is no escape for me. No escape at all."

"Why don't you turn over all the information you have to this government, Talya, and ask for protection? It's been done before."

She frowned at me. "Maybe later I could. But not now. It is too big a chance to take, to take positive action *against* my country. Now I merely want to be a nobody. Just a girl who sells frocks. I want to be on neither side. Can you understand that?"

There was a look of pleading in her green eyes. Strangely enough, I could understand what she meant.

"And why do you tell me?" I asked.

She straightened her shoulders. "I owe you that much, Dillon Bryant. You helped me. You helped someone who could just as easily have killed you."

"What did your friends say about the woman who had the data?"

"Just that she had been killed."

"By them?"

"It is possible. They did not say. My contact seemed most upset. The Union of Soviet Socialist Republics treats failure very harshly. He merely said that it was possible that you might have the data."

"And they still don't know."

"So you must be very careful. The ones who guard you are not enough. This is important enough so that great risks can be taken by my people."

"I have no data. What do these names mean to you? Ernst Haussmann. Tilda Renner."

She shook her head. "They mean nothing to me."

"You know, of course, that I should turn you over to my government."

Her shrug was expressive. "I would tell them nothing. They would most probably deport me. And I would be punished by my people."

"Will you describe your contact?"

"That can do no harm. He is about thirty. Sandy hair. Sunburned face. That sort of face in which you can read nothing. He has made himself very American."

It sounded like the one Jill had seen, and the one Laura had looked at from the third-floor window.

"Do you know where he works?"

"I do not even know the name he uses here. He is the one who must find me, or be condemned for an additional failure."

"Where did you report to him?"

"In a cafeteria on Canal Street." She made a wry face.

"It hurts even to speak of a cafeteria, I am so hungry."

I checked the kitchen. There was a can of beans. She heated them and I sat across the kitchen table from her and watched her eat them hungrily. Her fatalistic acceptance of what would happen to her was like a stone wall.

"Aren't you even going to try to make a run for it?" I asked.

She shrugged. "I am guilty. I *should* be punished."

"Think of my angle. I go out on a limb to find you a hideout. Then you want to walk out and take it in the neck. Seems like you wasted my time, doesn't it?"

She looked at me. "You've been very kind, Dillon Bryant."

"But your mind is made up?"

"I will go back to the shop tomorrow morning. This morning, I guess it is."

She took the plate over to the sink. I sat and watched her. I remembered all I had read of the Russians being an Oriental race. She was certainly an enigma. I told myself that it was of no emotional importance to me whether she lived or died. But it did seem a waste. Her first reaction had been to run, to hide. Now she wanted to sacrifice herself. Bryant, the poor man's psychiatrist. Bryant, missionary for life.

I went up behind her and put my hand on the curve of her waist, my arm around her. "When you're dead, Betty, you're dead a long time."

She gave me a quick, startled look. "Please don't," she said.

As she moved away from me, I caught her wrists. Her hands were wet from the tap. She twisted her wrists against my thumbs and broke free easily. She backed into the kitchen corner and I moved over to stand in front of her. Her eyelids half covered the green eyes. There was a completely Slavic impassivity about her.

I put my hands on her shoulders. "It's a nice thing to be alive," I said.

Under stress her voice thickened, an accent becoming perceptible. "Do what you want with me. Maybe I owe it to you."

Her eyes didn't waver away from mine. I let my hands drop to my sides. I stepped away from her. "Not that way," I said. "I'm having nothing to do with Talya. Nothing. I was just intrigued for a little while by a girl named Betty."

I walked through into the living room and to the door. She followed me, her bare feet noiseless on the carpet. I glanced at her feet. They had a peasant broadness, yet the arch was high. Her ankles were sturdy and the calves swelled into ripeness.

"I'll take the keys," I said. "When you leave in the morning make sure the lock snaps."

I opened the door. She still had not spoken. "Luck," I said, and started to walk out.

She caught my right wrist in both hands and pulled me back. She was strong. She put one bare foot high against the door and slammed it shut with a noise as loud as a pistol shot. She stood and looked directly at the third button of my shirt. Her lips had a swollen look.

"This is Betty," she said.

"No favors, Talya. No gratitude. No giving the boy a break."

"I told you it's Betty."

"You owe me nothing. I take stray dogs to vets. I find homes for kittens. They don't send me scrolls."

Her eyes lifted slowly. Second button, first button, chin, lips, nose. They steadied at my eyes. Her underlip stood out like a shelf. The wide heavy cheekbones gave her face a sullen triangularity. She was all woman, and yet the smaller tendrils of her hair, curled at the temples, gave her somewhat the look of a child. Her eyes steadied on mine and slowly the jet of the pupils grew, crowding the brown-flecked green iris, as though she looked into darkness. Lost lamb. Little lost lamb who had followed the wrong flock and found, now, that the crowded ramp led not to green pastures, but the cold practiced stroke of the executioner. Nothing is so forlorn as a fanatic who suddenly ceases to believe.

In the bedroom the fan whirred. It turned its whirling face blandly from side to side, in metronome idiocy. Its moist hot breath plucked at the empty sleeve of the lime and white dress. She was peasant-built. Thick round thighs, heavy bones, pelvic width, the incredibly narrow waist, and the flatness of peasant girlhood.

There was something oddly rustic about it all. Haymow. Barn warmth. An eagerness so elementary and so basic and so sweet. In comparison, Laura's had been a contrived and sophisticated passion, full of languid tricks and symbols. They had superimposed on this girl a series of political hates and prejudices. The flaw in all that was her basic nature—woman, bearer of children. She went back to that. Back to directness and simplicity and an enormous and natural urgency.

She was strong. She was steel springs. She cried out, not in tones of pain or anguish, but with the sort of sound she might have made if, rounding some mountain corner, she saw spread out below a fertile and beautiful valley. And then she wept for all the lovers in the world, and then she slept as a child sleeps.

Much of physical love is meaningless. It is an erotic spasm that does not touch the heart or soul, and leaves one feeling soiled and disdainful. When indulged in as Don Juanian conquest, it is but a meager victory. As the executioner winds the guillotine blade high and sees the trembling of the victim, his heart beats faster. Then the blade drops and he stares at the head in the basket, faintly ashamed that now he feels nothing.

That is the way it could have been—should have been —with Talya. Except for her directness, that is the way it would have been. Simplicity is the master of all subterfuge. I watched her sleep and felt a great tenderness toward her. Not love and not pity. In the slant of the light there was a faint sheen of perspiration on her body. Her lips were parted so that the light made a highlight of her lower lip and glinted on the visible edge of her white teeth. A strand of the dark blonde hair was curled around her throat.

It made me remember something I had forgotten for many years. When the first stirrings of adolescence came, I used to have strange fancies about a postage stamp. A special stamp from Spain. A reproduction of a painting of the Duchess of Alba. The Duchess and I were poorly matched participants in many waking dreams.

I dressed quietly without disturbing her. I made a neat bundle of her clothes, all of them, and took them into the living room and wrapped them up. I carried them out under my arm. I didn't want one Betty Morin to report to a dress shop in the morning. I wanted Betty Morin to run like hell and find a small town and a nice guy and forgetfulness.

As I walked through the sticky night I found that I was grateful to Betty-Talya. I remembered reading of a medical treatment. To cure one disease they inject you with the virus of another. The induced disease brings with it a fever that helps knock off the germs of the original disease. It gives the antibodies a better chance to function. In that sense, Talya had helped cure another phase of Laura. It was like opening a window to clear a smoky room. You see, Laura had never wept. Not once. For the first time I realized that Laura had been a woman quite beyond tears.

It was another faltering step in my uncertain progress toward a genuine maturity. I had kept a large slice of adolescence right up through and beyond thirty. I had remained a "big boy." Not quite the kind of big boy that goes around at Legion conventions goosing strange females with an electric stick and making paper-bag bombs, but a big boy none the less. Maturity implies the acquisition of a philosophy that not only functions, but that makes life satisfying. I didn't have it yet. But I felt that I was closer.

Chapter Eight

I DID NOT go back to the apartment. I took a cab out to an all-night drive-in on Gentilly Road. It was after three when I talked a frowsy, sleepy woman into renting me one of the glossy cubicles in her motor court, even if I didn't have a car. She charged me Mardi Gras rates.

It was a good shower and a good bed. One dream woke me up. That one about Laura being pulled into the boat on a hook and flopping naked on the floor boards. The guide still kept insisting that she was inedible. I lay sweating in the darkness and wondering about fish symbolism.

When I walked out of the court on Saturday at eleven in the morning, the sky had a funny, brassy look. The sun was twice the size it should have been. It was an ominous day. The speeding chrome on Gentilly winked and twinkled in the heat waves. There wasn't the slightest breath of wind. I hadn't gone back to the apartment because I wanted to avoid the effort of shaking off my playmates come Saturday evening. I decided they must be pretty irritated with me.

After a vast breakfast in an air-conditioned place, I walked back out into the simmer. It was one of those days when people speak in tired soft voices, and then explode into fits of violent and unreasonable anger. Even though it wasn't a day for thinking, I tried to sort out some kind of reasonable pattern in my mind. Laura had been killed either by Haussmann, by Talya's friends, or by an unknown party. So far, Talya's friends looked like the best bet. Motive—acquisition of the important data acquired by Laura in the Eastern Zone of Germany. Opportunity—Jill's description of the man across the street matched Talya's description of her contact.

The thing that clinched it in my mind was the attempt

made on me, the one that fell through because of Talya's softness. If Talya's friends had killed Laura, then they would be the only ones to know that the search hadn't been successful. Either Talya's contact had done it, or he knew who had done it. The search had been unsuccessful, and I didn't have the stuff they wanted. So where did it go? Had she memorized it? If so, it had died with her. If not, Haussmann was a good bet to have it. He was too conspicuous to do much running. So his safest bet was to hide out in the Quarter. After the fuss died down, he could make his own attempt to dicker with our government.

The whole business of crucial data and foreign agents would have been a lot less real to me were it not that I had seen some and sensed a lot more of the sort of thing going on in Venezuela while I was there. And in Mexico. And in all the free nations of the world. The days of brave armies with pennons and bugles are over. Now the trick is to plant your own people in the right spots. Have them ready to hamstring the opposition when the shooting war starts. New Orleans was a fine place in which to spot agents. A busy port is pretty vulnerable. And, with all the ship traffic, it makes a good relay point for information. I suspected that our team probably had a good line on a lot of the cells operating in this country, and that a pretty massive roundup would take place on the eve of the shooting war. It is better to let them alone and hope that they will lead you to the top boys than to grab them off and drive the top boys into deeper hiding.

Suddenly I wanted to see Talya again. Get a little more information. And a little more of Talya. There was a florist down the block. I went in with the idea of buying her something traditional. I came out with a hell of a big box of cornflowers. They seemed right for her somehow.

I took a cab to within a block of the apartment, then walked to a store and picked up some food. With my three bundles I went back to the apartment. I had to set them down to get the key in the lock. I opened the door and picked up the stuff and shouldered my way in, yelling, "Anybody home? Any ice today, lady?"

The lady didn't want any ice.

They lady was all through wanting anything.

She was face down over the footboard of the bed. The footboard cut across her at the hips. I had forgotten about Paul Harrigan's spare clothes. She had on a white shirt of his, the sleeves rolled up, and a pair of his khaki shorts, so big for her that the bottoms of them came below her knees. Her arms were stretched out ahead of her, and her still hands clutched the sheet. I found the tiny bloody spot at the nape of her neck. He had come behind her and had forced her over in that position and had held her there while he made the careful thrust.

The round empty face of the fan turned back and forth, back and forth. It was a fatuous after-dinner speaker, surveying his audience.

I told her that it was all right. I told her that it didn't hurt a bit. I kissed her temple. The tendrils of the dark blonde hair were still damp. Her knees were slightly bent and her bare feet had the soles upturned. They were dusty from the floor.

I put the flowers on the bed, the food in the kitchen, the bundle of clothes on a chair. I walked out of there and pulled the door shut. The lock clicked.

I think I wore a grin like you find on a skull. I was telling myself that the mortality rate among my women was too high.

I found a phone booth. Sam Spencer was in, and who is calling please, and just a moment, please.

"Dil? What's up? What's going on?"

"Sam. Just listen. Carefully. Listen carefully and give me a careful answer."

"You sound funny, boy."

"Shut up, Sam. You knew I got the apartment keys. I knew it. One other person knew it. But who else, Sam? Who did you tell?"

"Goddamnit, stop yelling in my ear. Captain Paris' office called. They had to get hold of you. It was very urgent. They wondered if I knew where you were. So I told them about the keys."

"Nobody else, Sam?"

"Not a soul. Not nobody. And I don't like the tone you're—"

I hung up on him. I called the police. It took ten minutes to be connected with Barney Zeck. "Who is this speaking?" he asked.

"Bryant. Look, Lieutenant, I—"

"Jesus, Bryant! Where are you? There's a general call out for you. You're to be picked up on sight. We're cooperating with a federal agency on that. Drag your tail on over here."

"No. I'm calling you back from another pay phone in ten minutes. Find out something. Find out if Captain Paris called Sam Spencer and asked where I was. Get me the answer and I'll tell you something interesting."

"Now, wait and—"

I hung up on him. I sat at the fountain and had a drink. Ten minutes later I called back on the same phone.

"No, Bryant. No such call was made. Why?"

"Somebody used Paris' name to find out where I was. They went to the address Sam gave them. They didn't find me, but they found somebody else. A girl. They killed her. That makes it your business, doesn't it?" I gave him the address.

"My God, Bryant! What kind of a—"

"You'll find my prints all over the place, but I didn't do it."

I hung up and got out of there. I didn't want to go near the Quarter. Not yet. And the city wasn't safe. The boys had got annoyed at me for giving them the slip. They wanted me on ice. They didn't want to use me as a stalking horse any more. The horse wouldn't obey orders, so lock him in the barn.

I found a phone booth in a corner cigar store. I had to use friends if I wanted to hide until dark. Movies would be no good. They'd watch the movies. I phoned Tram Widdmar's office. He was out and they didn't know when he'd be back. I tried his home. Same story.

Jill was at the paper. As soon as I spoke, her crisp voice softened. "Dil, I've been so worried."

"I need help, Jill. I need a place to hide out until this evening. How about your apartment?"

"Of course. And I want to talk to you. About a thing

that just came in. A dead girl. In Paul's apartment. Dil, what do you know about that?"

"If I don't tell you, will you still let me invite myself to your place?"

"Don't be silly. You're not a lady-killer of that particular variety. I'm going to be busy on this new thing. I'll have to send you the keys. I'll send them by a copy boy with flaming red hair and a bad case on me. Where will he meet you?"

"Right across the street from the St. Charles Theatre. In fifteen minutes."

"He'll be there, Dil. I'll come back to the apartment after I turn in my copy on this. Something tells me I won't have much copy. Someone is putting the lid on this whole affair."

Her apartment was deep in the Quarter, on Ursulines, in the heart of what was once upon a time the elite Creole section, and not far from the federal prison. An artist had lived in the apartment; had remodeled it, in fact. Jill took it over when he died. The location makes it inexpensive. As a ground-floor apartment it has its own tiny private court, with a bulbous bronze cupid leering and holding aloft the nozzle of a feeble little fountain. That cupid had always reminded me of Tram Widdmar. The street door is an ancient arched door of wide planks with a tiny view hole cut into it.

I let myself in and felt safe almost at once. The narrow stone hallway leads down to a second door, which is ironwork, open and lacy. Beyond that door is the huge livingroom-studio, with a wall of glass that frames the court and the cupid. The bedroom and bath are to the left, the kitchen and dining area to the right. No other occupant has windows that front on the court. Only in the old New Orleans construction, or in the homes of Latin America, can you find that wonderful sense of seclusion. Latin America is mystified by our Yankee insistence on building homes in such a way that any passerby can gawk in, by our lawns that are public gardens.

There was beer in the icebox. I opened a bottle and sat in the studio, staring out at the fountain. After a time I turned the valve and the cupid began to get sprinkled.

The thick stucco walls and tile floors kept the apartment cool inside. I put a stack of records on the turntable and adjusted the volume low.

The sudden interruption of the music woke me up with a start. I stared blankly at Jill Townsend. She wore a plastic apron over a two-piece sun suit of pale blue linen. She held the records in her hands and smiled at me. "When it repeated the third time I began to get nervous, Dil, and eight repeats was much too much."

"How'd you get in? How long you been here?"

"Two keys and almost two hours. Answer your questions?"

I stood up and stretched and yawned. Naps always give me a tar-paper mouth. I looked at my watch. Quarter to five. Drinking time.

"You'll probably get a jail term for this," I said.

"Scotch on the rocks? Or are you still on tepid gin and orange bitters?"

I shuddered. "Please. The Scotch."

"I'm going to give you enough Scotch to make you babble like a brook, my good man."

It was shady in the little court, and had been shady long enough for the stones to have cooled from the sun's heat. She came out with drinks, minus apron, and sat across the round wicker table from me.

"Now about the wench who got it in the neck?" she said. She was watching my face. "I'm sorry," she said quickly in a different tone. "Friend of yours, I judge."

"Friend of mine," I said, and stared at the leer on the cupid.

"It all smells, Dil. Here's what we get. No more. A store clerk named Elizabeth Morin was found dead in the empty apartment of an oil-company engineer who is out of the country at this time. Report of her death was made to the police through an anonymous phone call. Her presence in the apartment has not yet been explained. And that's all, Dil. Every bit of it. There were some nice neat bright young men around with that Washington file-cabinet look. Who was she, Dil?"

"Here's the only thing I can tell you, honey. I made a promise to some of those bright young men. They told me something in confidence. I can't tell you anything about the girl without opening up a lot of other things. All I can tell you is that she was a good kid. A very mixed-up kid. And a kid who didn't follow orders, and that is why she happens to be dead."

She set her glass down. "Now listen to me a minute. I'm no ball of fire, Dil, but I *can* add, a little. I know that all of this is big and bad and dangerous. I can *smell* that much. I have contacts. I know the local ropes. You, Dil, have got more muscles than caution. I don't want you to get your head knocked in. Promise or no promise, I think you'd better tell me. It won't get into the paper. This is just you and me. Jill and Dil. The kids that rhyme "

"Maybe I should have sought shelter with Tram I couldn't find him, though." As soon as I said it, I was sorry that it had slipped out. For a moment there was a quick hurt look in her gray eyes. She recovered quickly.

"O.K., my boy. I won't use a can opener on you. If you want to talk, go ahead. If not, you're still a guest."

I reached over and took her hand. "I shouldn't have said that."

"That's all right."

"Not completely all right. Be truthful."

She looked at me and I saw the tears begin to form, hanging heavy on her lower lids, ready to break free. She stood up with a quick smile. "Who am I to think I should own you just because I can help you? Fresh drink?"

I nodded. She walked off with quick steps. Her back was very straight. She carried her shining dark head high. I had never noticed before how sharply pronounced was the crease down her back, running between her shoulder blades. Only after it reappeared below the pale blue linen bra top were the tiny pebbles of the vertebrae visible. A small girl, but only in relation to others. Everything about her was in scale. Where Talya had been sturdy, Jill was patrician-slim, yet warmly ripe in her own subtle way.

I was still thinking of Jill in relation to Talya, and conjecturing about Jill in a way that I never had before, when she came back with the fresh drink for me. Some of what I was thinking must have shown on my face. She blushed faintly and sat down very quickly. It was odd that the death of Talya should start me thinking of Jill in this new, much more personal way. She had always been just . . . Jill. A good egg. A lot of laughs. I enjoyed her oblique outlook on life. But entirely a brother-sister pitch, and understood as that, even to the peck on the cheek at parting.

"How old are you, Jill?"

Her eyes widened. "Twenty-six. Why?"

"I don't know. It has occurred to me that you are a very handsome specimen."

"With this lopsided face?"

"Lopsided, hell! Piquant. Pixy. Tart. But not lopsided. No, I was just wondering why you haven't gone and got yourself married."

She gave me a mocking look. "Mine, sire, is a sad tale of unrequited love. I thrust my heart at yon yokel and he spurned it with jokes and laughter."

"A pretty stupid-type guy, eh?"

She put her chin on her fist. "When I was a sprout, lad, I had a dog-eared old cat named Oliver. Other people fed him, but he loved me. Just me. Very flattering. Who else had a one-woman cat? Nobody. I thought it made Oliver very special, and, incidentally, me too. They sent me away to school. Oliver gave it a fictional finish. He just pined away. No old blunt head rubbing on my leg any more. No big purr like a busted sewing machine. No kneading with the feet. Now for the moral. If Oliver had been capable of spreading his affection around, he would have been a well-adjusted cat. But as cats go, Oliver was psychotic. And I think he influenced my early years. I cannot spread myself around. All I can do is work like hell and try to forget the guy."

"Ever put it up to him?"

"Nope. Never will. And I've never even told anyone about him before, Dil. And I won't tell you his name, because you'd try to go running after him and pound some sense into his thick head."

"I'd do exactly that," I said.

"You said you wanted to hide out until tonight. What goes on tonight?"

"Call it a party."

"Can girls come?"

"There'll probably be some there, but I can't take you. I may not even be able to find the party."

She stared at me. "You've got a line on Haussmann, haven't you?"

"Haussmann? Who's Haussmann?"

"When you lie, your nose wrinkles up and your eyes go all bland and silly, Dil."

"I'd just like to know where you got that name."

She gave me an enigmatic smile. "Hell, son. Can't a girl have contacts too? I'm going off to cook. When you need a fresh one, come out in the kitchen." At the doorway she turned and said, "Barney confides in me sometimes."

Chapter Nine

WHEN dinner was almost ready, Jill went off and changed. I helped her move the table over to where we could look out on the little court as we ate. The deep shadows beyond the tarnished bronze of the cupid were blued and purpled by the approach of dusk. In the center of the table she put a slender white candle in a simple wrought-iron holder. The flame was motionless. She had changed to a simple white dress that left her shoulders bare. Her skin was like cream. I had to force myself to stop looking at her. This sort of thing wouldn't do at all.

The meal was simple. Two small steaks, a green vegetable, a tossed salad. It was much too hot to eat more.

"Tell me more about Barney confiding in you, Jill."

"Is it fair for you to pump me? And not tell me anything?"

"Now, listen. I want to be serious for a moment. You warned me that this was a big, rough situation, where I might get hurt. I don't like your knowing that name

Haussmann. I don't like your digging around too much, Jill."

"It's my business. I make my living at it."

"But you said yourself that the lid has gone on this thing. You can't print what you find out anyway. So why not drop it?"

"I am a very stubborn girl, Dil. Surprisingly stubborn. Maybe I can't print it right away. Someday I'll be able to. That's good enough for me. And—well, it's sort of a game to take the few facts you know, and try to make a picture. It's like a jigsaw puzzle where the rules permit you to manufacture a few pieces here and there. Can I talk about Laura without your getting all huffy with me?"

"Sure."

"The moralists say that no one is completely good or completely bad. And yet, Dil, I'm almost willing to say that Laura was bad. Call it a consciousness of evil. I don't blame you. She had her act polished well enough to blind any man. And you never saw her unless the act was in operation. I did, once. That last time. If you can say that a woman, just by her attitude, can turn a perfectly ordinary room into a sort of jungle, then Laura could do it. If and when this Haussmann is found, I think we'll find him to be a sort of male Laura."

The steak seemed to have lost some of its flavor. "How about Laura being the dupe of Haussmann?"

"Maybe when Laura was twelve or thirteen she was somebody's dupe, Dil. But not since that time, and not for long then."

"Did my—other friends all feel the same way?"

"Maybe not as strongly, but just about the same way."

"Couldn't you have stopped me?"

"With a detachment of Marines, or a bullet in the head. Perhaps. Look, Dil. Anything any of us said to you would have been like dropping a match in the gas tank. You were, as we old hillbillies call it, sot in your ways. We could hope it would blow over. But it didn't."

"A funny thing," I said. I watched the candle waver as my breath touched it. "I can't be sorry I married her. In some funny way it means growing up. Entering man's estate or something. New set of values. There's still anger left, but frankly, Jill, not a hell of a lot of sorrow. More sorrow for a girl who sold dresses."

"She was part of it all. She had to be part of it all. Paul's apartment and everything. Who was she with, Dil? Whose team was she on?"

"I can tell you that much, I guess. Mr. Stalin's team."

I watched her, expecting to see a slight bulge in the eye department, a look of shocked incredulity. Instead she looked as though she had suddenly put on a mask. A mask that looked like Jill Townsend, but was as dead and expressionless as a clever device made of rubber and plastic.

"No reaction?" I asked.

"Don't do anything—silly tonight, Dil. Can I come with you?"

"No."

"Take the key I sent you. You can get back in here. I may not be home."

"Where will you be?"

"Oh, investigating. That's a good couch there, if you want to use it. Comfortable. And you may need to stay out of touch for a while."

"Why?"

"Barney Zeck confides in me. He says a lot of people are annoyed with you, Dil. They think you'll be more predictable behind bars. And if they give Captain Paris his head, he thinks he can make the killing of that girl stick."

I stared at her. "Me? He thinks I——"

"I make my guests help with the dishes, pal. Bring out all you can carry."

It was full night by the time we were done. A bit after nine. She walked me slowly to the door. She put her fingertips on my arm. "You will be careful, Dil?"

"Shy as a mouse."

She went onto tiptoe to kiss me on the cheek. Her lips were cool. "The best of luck," she whispered.

Zeck had said that the little affair would take place somewhere within a two-block radius of the Café Lafitte. That sounded like a small area. It figures out to sixteen square blocks of the Quarter. From Governor Nicholls Street four blocks south to St. Ann. From Burgundy Street four blocks east to Chartres Street. Each block has four sides. Sixty-four streets one block long. The area included everything from very fancy private homes to sodden, murky little bars. It is not a brightly lighted area. The life and color were much farther south, toward Canal. That early, the people were taking advantage of the illusive coolness of the night air. The coolness was largely a delusion. Slow voices were resonant on the galleries. Groups sat on the steps off the banquettes, and fans waved slowly in front of pallid faces. Later, when that part of the city slept, I knew that my heels would make sharp echoes in the deserted streets. I avoided walking directly under the street lamps. When I was forced to do so, I kept my head lowered.

I saw a likely chance sitting on a low step in a doorway. Her blonde hair had a greenish glint. She wore a sheer blouse, a tight skirt. I paused and looked at her. She returned the stare steadily. There is no more red-light section in the Quarter.

I moved over and offered her a cigarette. She took it without a word. When I held the match I saw what the darkness had concealed. Deep pits in her cheeks and her nose. She looked up at me through the flame light.

"Pretty hot," I said.

"Wanta come inside? Got some beer on the ice."

"Beer sounds good," I said.

She got up with a small grunt of effort. She was taller than I had realized. Her posture was bad. Shoulders slumped forward, belly outthrust. I followed her down a narrow, damp-smelling corridor to a bedroom that faced a court. An ancient lift-top soft-drink box had been repainted, but the brand name still showed through. She lifted the lid after she turned on the light. The ice was nearly gone. The box was half full of water. Butter floated on a tin dish and she picked it out and set it out of the way.

She lifted a wet bottle out, deftly hooked the cap off on the side of the box, and handed it to me. I wiped the neck on my palm and tilted it up. The cold beer tasted good. She took a bottle too, closed the lid, and backed up until the backs of her knees struck the bed. She sat down. It was an old bedstead turned into a "Hollywood" bed by sawing off the posts and most of the legs.

"What's your name, honey?" she asked.

"Joe."

"Got a present for Christy, Joe?"

I set the beer bottle down on top of the soft-drink case, took a five out of my wallet, and floated it onto the bed beside her hip. "Not enough, Joe," she said metallically.

"Enough for what I want. I just want this beer and a little talk."

"You just want a little talk. You got words you want me to say to you? Once a guy had them all typed out for me to read to him."

"I want information."

She stiffened. "I told you guys before. I haven't seen him in two years. Why don't you catch him and stop bothering me?"

"I don't know what you're talking about, Christy. Look, I heard there's a show around this neighborhood someplace. I heard it's within a few blocks of here. But I can't find it."

She gave me a look of contempt. "Oh, you're one of those, eh?"

"Is there a law against it?"

"I say everybody is the way they are, and what can you do about it?"

"That's a sound philosophy. Where's the show?"

She bit her lip and frowned. "Gee, honey, I don't know. But look, I got a friend. I could call her from the corner."

"Does she know where it is?"

"No, but she's got quite an act of her own. Me, I don't go for that sort of thing. Will that do? It'll only cost you another twenty. Maybe she could come right over."

"No. I want to find the one I heard about."

"It runs steep, honey. Maybe a hundred bucks."

73

"That's all right."

"I sure wish I could help. I know where it *used* to be, before it was raided and they jailed everybody. But they keep it awful quiet."

"How did you used to steer people when you knew where it was?"

"They had to go to a place called Kobel's. That's two blocks over. And get Jimmy the bartender aside and ask him where to find Dagwood." She giggled. "Hell of a name, isn't it?"

"But that's changed?"

"Oh, sure. But say! I bet you Jimmy might know, at that. He's got a scar. A bad one. It pulls his mouth up. They say a girl dug him with a pair of scissors while he was out cold, and he damn near bled to death."

"Thanks, Christy, and thanks for the beer."

"That's O.K. Look, if you get disappointed, you come back and I'll call my friend. She's real pure Creole and cute as anything."

She came out with me. When I looked back she was sitting on the step again. I walked to Kobel's. You went down one step from the sidewalk to get into it. It was the sort of place that makes the hair on the back of your neck crawl. Even though it wasn't logical, you had the feeling that you could get your throat cut for fifty cents in there. Very probably the worst that could happen would be a micky and then a roll job in the nearest alley. I was glad of the blue-black shadow of beard on my throat and jaw. A few men sat at tables. Several stood at the bar.

I went down to the far end of the bar near a stone doorway that led into a dingy back room. There was no music. There was no conversation. Just those men, each sunk in his own particular and special hell.

I had no doubt that the bartender was Jimmy. I would have guessed at hedge clippers rather than scissors. The scar started under his right eye and slanted down to his mouth. The lip was pulled up so high that it lay against the side of his snub nose, and left three gold-capped teeth permanently exposed. It gave him a whistling speech defect.

"Can of beer," I said. He named some brands. I picked one. I watched his hands carefully as he jacked holes in the top of the can. It was that sort of place. I laid a five on the bar. As he reached casually for it I said in a low voice, "Keep the change, Jimmy."

His hand was a plump ocher spider that stood poised on stubby legs over the bill. "Who are you?"

I hunched forward. "I was wondering where Dagwood hangs out these days."

He leaned forward and whispered, "Ain't you a little out of date, pal?"

"I haven't been in town for some time."

"Dagwood ain't around no more, pal."

"Who's holding down his job?"

Velvet eyes with surprisingly long lashes dropped significantly down to glance at the bill. I added a twin to it. The plump spider sucked them up and whisked away with them. "Guy named Abner took his place."

"How do I find Abner?"

"This is no guarantee, pal. They got to take a look at you. And you're early. Right about midnight, a little before, you go up to the corner. Take a right. Halfway down the block is a warehouse, on the far side of the street. There's a picket fence with a green gate just beyond the front of the warehouse. Rap on that green gate. Anybody answers, you're looking for Abner. Have your dough ready, too. One hundred bucks on the line."

"How is it?"

"When would I have a hundred bucks, pal?"

A man signaled down the bar. Jimmy went down to take care of him. I finished the beer and walked out. I didn't feel at ease on the street. A cruiser that went by, decal on the door, didn't help any. I had the feeling they were going to flick on the spot and pin me against the wall like a bug on a board. I was sweating more than the heat excused by the time the cruiser turned down the next street. I followed Jimmy's directions and oriented myself in respect to the green gate. The picket fence was only about ten feet long, and too high to see over. No light showed through the pickets.

I had no choice. I could either hang around and wait

for the distinctive silhouette of Haussmann, or I could go on in. They wouldn't be such fools as to leave the street unwatched. Hanging around might turn out to be exceedingly unhealthy. And there was the additional factor that Haussmann might enter by some other way. It wasn't likely that such a setup would depend on only one entrance and exit.

By my watch it was almost eleven. One hour to kill. I walked a block and a half to the Café Lafitte. I walked by, slowly, and looked through the windows that front on the sidewalk. There were several groups of customers, and one burly man who stood alone next to the open fireplace in the middle of the room. I didn't care for his looks, for his air of endless patience. Police patience, it seemed. I kept right on walking, right down Bourbon. At the first bar that looked dimly lighted, I turned in. I found a small table in the shadows. The waiter brought a Scotch. I nursed it along, made it last. The minutes seemed endless.

When at last it was time I left and headed back. I reached the green gate at ten minutes of twelve. The place seemed as deserted as before. I rapped. It was a lonely sound on the quiet street. Nothing happened. I wondered if Jimmy had made himself a fast ten dollars. Just as I started to rap again, the gate opened. The hinges had been well oiled. There wasn't a sound.

"What do you want?" a cold low voice asked.

"I'm looking for Abner."

"Step in. I'll see if he's here."

I stepped into a darkness like the bottom of a mine. No sound. A harsh white light blinded me. It clicked off and the darkness was greater than before.

"Who told you Abner might be here?"

"Jimmy."

The light came on again and was turned on me at waist level. Enough of it reflected from my shirt so that I could see the pale oval of a face behind the light, but I could make out no features.

"Count it out."

A fifty, two twenties, and a ten. He took the money. The light went out. In a matter of seconds soft footsteps approached. I guessed that some signal had been given. I was ordered to follow the new one. He took me back through darkness. My left hand brushed the shaggy wall of the warehouse. I didn't like any part of it.

Chapter Ten

IT WAS in the warehouse itself, on the second floor. We rounded a corner and ahead was a narrow aisle between packing cases, a light at the end of the aisle.

"Go in and find a seat," my guide whispered. "No talking."

I went slowly down the aisle. At first I could smell dust, a tang of rodents, a scent of mildew and damp rot. Then slowly a musky incense grew stronger. It did not cancel out the warehouse smell. It floated strongly on top of it, like a heavy sustained trumpet note riding on a dim rhythm beat.

The aisle led to an open space. Directly ahead was a raised stage. Two underpowered floodlights were mounted on the front edge of the stage, slanting back toward a dusty wine-colored backdrop that could have been the curtain from some movie house long extinct. I could get no clear idea of the size of the room. Just the impression of a high ceiling. I could feel expectancy around me, but I could not see the audience. I shut my eyes tightly for ten seconds, then opened them wide. It worked—a little. Audience chairs became visible. Little uncomfortable folding chairs. The kind that can be rented from undertakers.

The occupied chairs were merely heavier shadows. I moved up and found an empty chair. Slowly my vision improved. I saw that I was four rows from the improvised stage. Around me I could hear the stir of breathing, an infrequent rustle of cloth, the shuffle of feet, the scrape of a chair leg. On my right, two feet from my right hand, was the red glow of a cigarette end. It moved upward in a low arc to waiting lips. It brightened, made a pinkish glow on a face. A woman's face. It lasted just long enough for me to see that she was young, that she wore a black mask across her eyes. The cigarette went back down in the same slow arc.

There was nothing to do but wait. I tried to pierce the darkness and find the oversized shadow that might be Haussmann. A pair of new customers arrived. And then a single. And then a trio. They found chairs and settled themselves to wait. I counted the house. I couldn't be completely accurate, but it seemed to be more than thirty.

Better than three thousand dollars. As near as I could guess, there were ten chairs in each row, and six rows. A full house would bring in six thousand. It wasn't the sort of business you'd want to make tax declarations on.

Around me was sickness. A disease of the soul. I could taste it. Not an uncommon disease. Cans of movie film can be rented. Still pictures are distributed furtively. The market is always big. It seems strange that this should be so. It is the visual perversion of an elemental drive. It is filth. It is social cancer. I could sense the dry-mouthed waiting around me, the impatient thud of pulse.

When the man moved onto the stage there was a slow sigh from the darkness. He was a magnificent Negro, his body an oiled symmetric blackness, his heavy face full of the elemental and regal dignity of the Watusi. He wore a loincloth and a necklace of bone and feathers. A bright red stick pierced the central membrane of his nose, forcing the wide nostrils even wider. Across his gleaming chest were three broad bands of pale aqua. He carried a squat barbaric drum from which dangled heavy chains of copper coins, jangling faintly as he walked. He sat cross-legged in the center of the stage, his back almost touching the curtain, the drum in front of him. He looked out into the darkness with somber contempt.

The room grew very still. The man touched the drum lightly, the faint boom barely audible. And he touched it again, as though casually. After a long pause he tapped it twice in quick succession. Thus was the basic thread of the rhythm born. Slowly he increased the beat, and as he began to use more force, the strands of coins added their faint music. Comfort left his face as he began to lose himself in the increasing complications of the beat. His eyes grew glazed with concentration and lips pulled back from teeth that blazed white.

I had planned to be the objective observer. But that drumbeat reached back into that part of you that is forever a savage, that still dances on the jungle floor while beasts cry shrilly in the night. The rhythm took you out of objectivity and made you one with the sick pulse of those who sat near you in the darkness.

A woman spun into the light. She was as black as the man. Frantic white showed all the way around the pupils of her eyes, and the cords of her throat were taut. Her breasts were heavy, dark-nippled, her loins like the night. Every motion was built upon the drumbeat, was complementary to it, and the slap of her bare feet on the floor was a rhythmic offbeat.

The rhythm drugged me so that I barely noticed the second man who spun out into the night. I barely noticed the short stick, the whir of the three-thonged whip.

When the blow landed across the naked back, when the blood gleamed dark, it was as though someone had dashed ice water into my face. It brought me out of it, brought me back to shame that I could have been lost for so long. The blows continued to land, and nausea thickened in my throat. Once again I became conscious of the people around me as individuals instead of a dark entity. What had sobered me instantaneously seemed only to heighten their intense identification with the act. I remembered reading of the cult of the flagellants, of bloody Easters in the Sangre de Cristo Mountains. Not for me. Not ever for me.

I sat and fought physical illness as the frenzy on the stage continued, as more actors entered on cue, as unmentionable acts began to be mingled with the pain and the blood. I tried to keep my eyes turned away from the stage, but it was much the same as the horrid fascination of an open wound. To look at it makes you ill, and yet you cannot cease looking at it.

I grew abruptly aware of the masked woman at my

right when, with a low moan of torment, she began to clutch at me with her hands, began to writhe against me. I pushed her away with such force that she fell from the chair. No one seemed to notice. I began to detect other stirrings of sodden violence in the dark audience. The woman got up from the floor and plunged forward to the stage. Within an incredibly short time she was on the stage, wearing only the mask. She was spectator and participant. As I saw the manner of things that were being done to her, I dropped from the chair onto my hands and knees and crawled back into the greater darkness. With my face close to the dry wood of the packing cases, I was gaspingly ill. I got weakly to my feet and turned to look back at the stage. Strangely, it had lost the power to touch me. They were white and brown and black marionettes. They were not real. They could not be human beings. Just toys that writhed and jerked as the clever strings were pulled.

A voice said, close to my ear, "Soon it will be over. You can leave now, if it makes you sick. The others will leave, one by one, in the darkness."

"I'll wait until it's over," I said thickly. The stranger moved away. After enduring all this, I could not stand the thought of missing Haussmann. But if it remained dark, I would never find him.

And then I got the idea. The only way I could pick out Haussmann was to get between him and the lights. The back row of seats was empty. I took the one on the end and slumped down to bring my eyes on a level with the back of the chair in front of me. The fourth chair I tried disclosed a massive silhouette two rows in front. I moved a bit to the side. They had told me his blond hair was worn long in back. The silhouette of the head matched. One more test. I moved up directly behind him. He sat like a stone image of a man, absolutely motionless, his eyes on the stage. I tipped over the chair I was sitting on, and rammed my shoulder against the back of his chair.

He turned his head sharply and in a high voice said, "Excuse me, please." It was accented. Not much. Not enough to be "Eggsguse me, blease," but with a bare suggestion of the memory of Weber and Fields. It was good enough for me.

Now I had to stick with him. And that might be more of a trick than I bargained on. The hour-long act had passed its crescendo. The stage crowd was thinning, and the drumbeat was subtly slowing. When he moved with surprising lightness and quickness for his great bulk, I nearly lost him in the darkness. He moved toward the left of the stage. I scrambled after him, careless of noise. He stopped and bent over a figure that lay on the floor in the darkness. At this angle the light was stronger on his face. I saw his blond hair. Some of the customers were beginning to leave. I saw him fumbling in the darkness and it took a few moments to figure out that he was gathering up garments. He lifted the figure by the stage, and I saw the mask across her eyes. She stirred weakly as he clumsily fitted the clothes on her slack body.

The drumbeat had dwindled almost into silence. Sweat had almost removed the aqua bands across the chest of the savage drummer.

In the silence I heard the woman say, "Who are you? Who are you?"

"Put your arms in the sleeves," Haussmann said.

"Who are you? What do you want?" Her voice was thin, querulous.

His shoulder moved a trifle and I heard the smack of a hard palm on flesh. "Be still. You come with me."

She made no further protest outside of the occasional thin whine. He got her to her feet just as the drummer stood up, picked up the drum, and stalked slowly into the shadows, his feet scuffling with weariness.

"Let me help you with her, sir," I said, hoping he'd mistake me for part of the management.

"Take her other arm," he said arrogantly.

"You came with her, of course, sir."

"Of course."

We walked her back around the chairs toward the beginning of the corridor between the packing boxes. The management said, "One at a time."

"We're helping this woman," I said casually.

"O.K. Get her out of the neighborhood as fast as you can."

"Take her," Haussmann said. He walked ahead, his shoulders almost brushing the packing cases on either side. I struggled along with the woman. She was like a rag doll. She was making feeble efforts to walk. I sweated and cursed her in whispers.

Outside the night air was a bit cooler. Someone held the green gate open and we went outside. Haussmann turned to the left and walked almost to the corner before he stopped and waited. As I came up he yanked her away from me.

"All right," he said.

"I want to go home," the woman whined. The street light was near enough so that I could see that her clothes were of good quality.

He shook her. "Shut up! I take you home."

"Who are you?" she asked forlornly.

"Please," Haussmann said to me, with a small bow from the waist. "You are not needed any longer."

I shrugged and walked back into the darkness. They went around the corner. I waited ten seconds, then hurried diagonally across the street and went up to the corner. He was hurrying her along. I could still hear her thin complaints. I followed them for a block and a half. He turned down a narrow alley. I risked a look. Thirty feet down the alley three wooden steps led up to a blue door. The woman sat on the bottom step, her head on her knees. Haussmann was inserting a key into a lock in the blue door. The door swung inward. He reached down and lifted her by one arm with effortless strength. The door swung shut, and as it clicked the low-wattage bulb over the door went out.

I went cautiously down the alley. A tin can rolled noisily as I kicked it. I froze. A cat made a hideous sound in the darkness and I nearly jumped out of my skin. I wanted to find some window I could look into. Three other doorways opened into the alley. I went to the end and found that it was blocked by a high stucco wall.

As I turned back I saw, outlined against the faint light of the street, the bulky towering figure of Haussmann.

"Who is there?" he called softly.

I did not answer.

He took three slow steps toward me. "Who is there?"

I sang to him. I made it ripe and slurred and off key. "You're the flow-ah of my hear-r-r-rt, Sweet Ad—o—line!"

He cursed softly in German and came toward me. A drunk to be tossed out into the street. I crouched against the wall. He reached carelessly for me. It had to be a lucky shot. I put everything I had into it. I put hate and fury into it. And all the sick distaste for what I had seen, and for the sort of people who watched it. I hit over and down, trying to catch the shelf of the jaw with maximum shock effect. It hit squarely and my arm went numb from knuckles to elbow. He grunted and braced his feet. His reaching arm sagged slowly to his side. He shook his massive head from side to side. I hit him again. It was a little high. He went back a half step, still shaking his head. Then the big arms began to come up. As they reached for me, I braced my shoulders against the wall, brought my knee up to my chest, then stamped out at his belly. It was like stamping against a tree. It drove him back two steps and he braced himself and moved in again, faster than before. It seemed incredible, but he was recovering. I had the hopeless feeling that he couldn't be stopped with an eight-pound sledge.

As he reached for my face, I slid down into a sitting position, tucked my knees under my chin, and then let fly at his knee. One foot glanced off. My right heel caught the kneecap. Once I heard a horse fall on the ice and give that same sort of soft whistling scream. As he fell he got his hands on my left leg, just above the ankle. My leg suddenly felt as if it had been caught between a boat and a dock. The sudden pain made me feel dizzy. I stamped my right heel at his face three times before his grip slackened. I tore away, rolled over and over, and came up onto my feet, panting.

He was a slow shadow crawling toward me, making a soft scraping sound in the rubble. I moved back and struck against a trash can. I lifted the lid off it by the handle, then turned it so that I grasped it by the edge.

I swung it high with both hands and brought it down on his head so hard that it lifted both my feet off the ground and made the flat metallic sound of a Mexican church bell. He didn't move again. I tried with shaking hands to put the lid back on the trash can. It was bent so that it wouldn't fit. I stumbled up the wooden steps. The blue door was ajar. It opened directly into a small room. There was a cot, a hot plate on a wooden shelf, a grass rug, one wicker chair. A door opened into a tiny bathroom with concrete floor. The woman sat on the bed. She lifted her bruised face from her knees as I came in. Her eyes were dull. The mask was on the floor.

I pulled her to her feet. "You can go now. You've got a chance to get out of here now." Blood had soaked through the pale back of her short light jacket. The side of her mouth was swollen and purple. She stumbled down the steps, turned toward the street, and broke into a wavering run, whining as she ran. I left the door open as I searched the room. I didn't know what I was looking for, or even why I was looking. Maybe he had what Laura had been killed for. I found nothing. No personal papers. Very few clothes. It gave me a crawling feeling to think of searching his unconscious body. I wiped my damp palms on the sides of my thighs.

I pulled the door almost closed and went into the alley and listened. There was no sound, no sign that the people behind the other three doors had heard anything. Possibly they had. And probably they knew better than to investigate any small-hour sound in the dark alley.

The stars overhead looked misty. I looked down at Haussmann. His forehead rested on his right forearm. His left hand was outstretched. I put my foot against his shoulder and shoved roughly. He was completely limp. I went down on one knee and found the side pocket of his jacket. Empty. The pocket on the other side was caught under him. I pulled it free. Also empty. I folded the tail of his jacket up over his waist. I worked a wallet out of his right hip pocket. Just as I had it free, the outstretched left arm swept back like a club and knocked my legs out from under me. I tried to fall toward him and get my arm around his bull neck.

But he rolled face up and clubbed me alongside the head as I fell. His big arms folded around my chest and his hands locked between my shoulder blades. He laughed low in his throat as he rolled on top of me. I tried to find his eyes and he buried his face against my throat. I hammered at the back of his head, but could get no force in the blows. I grasped for an ear and it slipped out of my sweaty hand. He put his brute strength into the crushing grip around my chest. Blackness was like a bird of night that swooped down at me. I sucked in air and tried to hold it. I felt two ribs go with separate little popping sounds. I could not see or hear or move. He said something cooingly to me in German, and I felt the air being forced out of my lungs, tearing through my throat.

A far-off voice said a single harsh word. Haussmann's muscles went slack. As I sucked in the air I felt the thin grate of the broken rib ends. I felt him go tense, and then his enormous weight was suddenly gone as he rolled away.

I heard him scramble through the rubble, knocking against the trash cans. I sat up. Enough light came through the crack of the blue door so that I could see the small fat man in a shabby suit who stood with the knife blade held directly in front of his belly, the point toward Haussmann.

The little fat man spoke in German. He took a few steps forward out of the light, into the shadows. I crawled to the steps and reached up and pushed the door back with my fingertips. I turned. I saw Haussmann reach the alley wall. With a tremendous effort he pulled himself up onto his one good leg. With his shoulders against the wall he put both hands out, palm upward.

"*Nein!*" he said shrilly.

The little fat man marched slowly forward. He spoke softly. He stood an arm's length from Haussmann.

"*Nein! Ach, lieber Gott . . .*"

The fat man swung the knife in low, ripped upward and backed quickly away. The knife no longer picked up highlights. Haussmann bent from the waist. He pressed his hands hard against himself. When it looked as though Haussmann would fall forward onto his face, the little man stopped the forward movement by placing his left hand against the top of Haussmann's head. He reached underneath Haussmann's face and pulled the knife quickly across the full throat, jumping back in the same movement to let Haussmann fall unimpeded. He bent over and wiped the knife, first one side and then the other, in two long strokes, across the broad expanse of shoulders.

He turned and stared at me. "Too quick," he said softly.

"I'm glad you came along when you did."

Suddenly he staggered again, I caught him. He leaned heavily against me and I got him up the steps into the room. I kicked the door shut and got him onto the cot. He lay on his back. The knife had fallen. It lay across the abandoned mask.

I found a jelly glass and got water from the bathroom tap. He had fumbled two pills out of his pocket. He put them in his mouth. A lot of water went on the front of his clothes, but enough went into his mouth to help get the pills down. He lay back. His color was ghastly. Slowly it improved and his breathing steadied.

He smiled at me. It was an oddly sweet smile. Very shy, very apologetic.

"You've got to get away from here," I said.

"It doesn't matter."

"I should be running right now. But I want to know who you are, and why you did that."

"A very simple story. And an unpretty one. My name doesn't matter. Anyway, I was not representing myself. I was representing thousands of others who also knew Herr Haussmann in—the old days. Graduates of Belsen, and Buchenwald, and Dachau. Herr Haussmann was Gestapo chief in my home city, Gummersbach, in the Rhineland. He recruited many of us for the camps. He and his whore. It was enough that you had something he wished. A bit of land. A shop. A painting. A daughter. He could make you confess. I had all four things he

86

wanted. Land, a shop, a Tintoretto, and a daughter. That filth took all of them. I confessed to being a traitor. My wife died in Belsen. But I lived. Somehow. I came here. And two weeks ago, on the street, in this country, in this city, walking in freedom, I saw Haussmann and his whore. Her hair had been dyed, but I knew her. My life is nearly over anyway. Bad heart damage from the years in the camps, from the forced labor. What would you do, my friend?"

"Did you kill the woman?"

"No. It would have been nice to kill her. But I do not even know if I could have brought myself to do it. Someone . . . killed her. I believe unpleasantly. This Haussmann I followed. I lost him. I gave up my work, everything, to find him again. Today I found this place. That is why I came back with a knife. I am glad it is done. But it was too quick. I meant it to be a lasting thing, for him to die slowly."

"What did you have against the woman?"

He sat up slowly. "Against her? I shall never forget. She came to call on us at our home. Oh, so very sweet. Twenty minutes after she left, the cars came. They searched our home. In the cushions of the chair where she had sat they found the little printed thing, the thing that made a lewd joke of Adolf. It was enough. The three of us, we were taken at once to her lover at the Gestapo headquarters of Gummersbach. There we were separated. I never saw my daughter again. I saw my wife once, though, beyond the wire at Belsen. That is what I have against the woman—that she smiled and talked and made a social visit to us, and in that way killed us."

My face felt as though Haussmann's blow had torn half of it away. I said, "You've got to get out of here. We've got to get out of here."

"It doesn't seem important."

"Come on. I'll help you."

His color still wasn't right. He compressed his lips and took a firm grasp on my arm. He came to his feet, wavering a bit.

"Steady, now," I said. "Take it easy."

Once again he gave me that quick, shy, oddly sweet smile. As the smile faded his eyes dulled. He sucked hard for air and his face slowly darkened. I tried to get him back to the cot, but his knees went slack and he slid out of my hands. It hurt my ribs to pick him up. I was afraid the broken end of one of them would punch into a lung. I got him on the cot. Then I straightened up and looked at him and knew at once that it had been a pointless effort.

I found the light switch and turned out the lights. I swung the door open and stood, listening. The cat screeched again, somewhere close at hand. A car purred by the mouth of the alley. Haussmann was a shapeless shadow near the wall. A siren called into the night, far away, receding. There was a taint of garbage in the air, and mingled with it the steamy smell of blood.

I looked into the darkness and saw a dark-haired Laura sitting in a cluttered European parlor, chatting brightly with the people who feared her. I tried to tell myself that Laura could have done no such thing. But it was no good. Because I could see her. Just as clearly as though I had been there.

I remembered the money. Laura's money. They say money has no memory. But I knew I could never touch it now. I could find out where to send it. It might do a little good, but it could never undo any of the harm. I walked out of the alley and into night air on the baked street, air like the breath from an animal's mouth.

Chapter Eleven

JILL was at her place. I got the outside door open. As I shut it behind me, she swung the wrought-iron door open and came down the hallway toward me. The light was behind her. She wore a loose robe and pajamas.

"At last the wanderer returns from— Dil! What happened? You're hurt!"

"I ran into a door, they tell me."

She held tightly to my wrist until I was safely seated in the living room. She said, "You're cut, too. I'll get the first-aid kit."

"What can you do for broken ribs? I seem to have a couple."

She stared down at me, her head cocked on one side, tapping her chin with a slim finger. She went back through the wrought-iron door to the phone stand, just beyond it. She turned on the hall light and looked at the book, then dialed crisply.

"Jack? Jill Townsend. How about a night call? No, you big wolf, it isn't for me. A house guest. With broken ribs, and a cut on his face. Yes, he tripped and fell. Thanks, Jack. See you."

He arrived in twenty minutes. He was a square-faced guy with tinted bifocals and a cheery look. He tapped Jill under the chin and bustled over to me.

"Off with the shirt, my friend." I got out of it painfully. He had me stretch out on the couch while he tapped and probed. "Nice clean breaks. There may be some cracked ones, too. I pity you in this hot weather." He took a big wide roll of tape, and he used it generously.

He put his finger over the area where the breaks were. "Deep breath. That's it. Any pain? Good. It'll bother you trying to get to sleep."

He washed the cut on my face with antiseptic solution and applied a small bandage.

"Warm weather to fall off roofs, my friend."

"Thanks so much for coming over, Jack," Jill said. "What do we owe you?"

"Ten ought to do it. Want me to bill you?"

I dug out ten and handed it to him. He turned to Jill. "Give him a couple of those sleeping pills of yours, if you've got any left, honey. You said he's a house guest?"

"That's right."

Dr. Jack looked hard at me. "Behave, my friend. You're staying with my girl."

"Want me to tell Josie about this, Jack?"

He winked at her. "I tell her every day. I keep saying, 'Honey, why don't you divorce me so I can marry that Townsend wench?' But she knows a good thing when she's got it. She won't let me go, not after getting me all housebroke."

"Time for a drink, Jack?" Jill asked.

"No. I got to go roll a few pills. If you have trouble, my friend, stop in at the office."

He bustled out. Jill walked him down the hall to the door. I heard the low murmur of their voices. I worked my way back into the shirt with certain difficulty.

She came back. "Like him? I think he's very special. How about a nightcap and some more conversation, Dil?"

She brought me Scotch on the rocks. She looked at me. "Dil, something has happened to you tonight. I can see it in your eyes. It's something that—isn't pretty to see."

"I'm considering a resignation from the human race."

"It's a sad tribe, Bryant. You may have something there. What would you like to be?"

"A nice, clean animal. Always had a soft spot for possums."

"Oh, they're the ones with the cute black bandit masks, aren't they?"

"Then I think we better skip possums."

She came over quickly and sat beside me on the couch. "I want to tell you something, Dil. Maybe I won't say it right. I don't want to sound like Pollyanna. The first dirty assignment I got in the newspaper game. A dirty-fingered amateur abortionist and a dead fourteen-year-old girl on a kitchen table in a tiny apartment over in Irish Channel. That was when I wanted to resign from the human race. It made me ashamed to be a member. I went around in a blue funk. My copy was flat and horrid. The girl cynic. And then there was another story. A fat lady tourist went trotting across the tracks. She was taking a short cut to catch her train. The porter was running after her with her bags. She jammed her foot in a switch. Couldn't pull it out. A switch engine was backing toward her, fast. The porter dropped the bags, got hold of her ankle, wrenched her foot out of the switch, and threw her bodily out of danger. He got his own left foot clipped off at the ankle. The lady didn't catch her train. She stayed in town until the porter got out of the hospital. She paid everything, deviled the railroad people into giving him a sitting-down job, got him fitted with a fancy artificial foot, and settled enough money on him so that he still gets a little income from it. It isn't much, but the tourist lady didn't have much. That sort of put me back in the human race, Dil. Nobody would have blamed him for jumping clear while he still had time."

"What does it prove?" I asked her.

"Nothing, I guess. Just that people are good and people are bad."

"Laura was bad. Not like the little girl with the curl— when she was bad she was horrid. Another kind of bad. Black bad. Stinking bad."

She took my hand in both of hers. She pressed hard. I suppressed a wince. The knuckles were swollen and sore. "Oh, Dil! You found out something, didn't you?"

I leaned back and closed my eyes. I was speaking more to myself than to her. I told about a girl named Tilda Renner, who paid a visit. I described the way it was, the way I could see it through the eyes of the fat little man who had died. I told about the fat little man, and what had happened to him when he had seen Tilda Renner and Ernst Haussmann walking safe and free on a New Orleans street, and how such a man could take justice into his own hands, knowing that most of the world had forgotten how it was with the fat little man. I left my own participation out of it. I told of the fat little man facing Haussmann, and the knife, and how, in that last moment, he had given Haussmann a quick and almost merciful death, only to die himself within fifteen minutes of the deed because of the strain on his damaged heart.

I opened my eyes then and looked at her. Tear tracks were shiny on her smooth cheeks. Her gray eyes were far away, in another year, in another time. "And Laura was Tilda Renner," she said softly.

"She was."

Suddenly Jill stiffened. "Say! I almost forgot my profession. The second oldest, they call it."

"The alley is dark. The odds are against anybody finding them yet."

"The lady goes to work, Dil."

"Now, wait a minute!"

"I can tip off Barney. Then, by the time I get there, the alley will be crawling with law."

"And won't Barney want to know how you happened to know?"

She frowned. "That's a point."

"And Barney will jump to the very reasonable conclusion that I was there and I came back and told you. That means I'll have to find me another refuge at three-something Sunday morning."

"But—"

"And the lid will be clamped onto this one just the same as with the girl in Paul's apartment, and you won't be able to write anything, anyway."

She sat down again and pouted. "Damn it, Dil, this sort of thing is news. And exclusive news, at that. If I could only—"

"Suppose I give you something you can really cover. Call it a trade. And you'll be doing some good in the world. You can't cover it tonight, but you can find out the right evening next week and blow a large hole in a very dirty and very profitable little venture. The cops are interested in it, but they haven't found it yet. Does it sound like a fair trade?"

"It better be pretty good, Dil. It better be as good as a murder."

"That's for you to judge." She paced back and forth in front of me, not looking at me, as I told her where to find Abner, told her how I got the lead, described the layout, and left the actualities pretty much up to her imagination. As I talked, the look of distaste and disgust grew stronger.

She took long strides for such a small girl. She stopped

and faced me. "I begin to understand why you're a little fed up with the human race. All that and Haussmann too."

"Is it good enough to take in trade? Is it good enough to cancel the call to Barney?"

"Let me do my pacing and my thinking, mate."

She frowned as she walked back and forth. I knew that she became unconscious of my presence. The light-weight, loosely belted robe slipped open. She hung a cigarette in the corner of her mouth, took a kitchen match from a brass dish on the coffee table, and popped it on her thumbnail. She trailed a cloud of smoke, and she looked like next year's debutante pretending to be a dead-end kid. Under the pajama top her breasts were high, conical, wide-spaced, quite startlingly abundant. I decided that for the few years I had known her, she must have been deceiving the public, and going around in considerable constriction and discomfort.

She stopped. "Dil, I am a kid who—" She glanced down quickly and yanked the robe around her and belted it firmly. "As I was saying, I am a kid who likes to have her cake and eat it too. Thanks for the information. I'm going to call Barney and ask him to meet me. I'm going to tell him that you phoned me and gave me a line on where Haussmann lives. That will put me in a position to cover it. I'll let Barney find the scene of violence, and I'll be there with my little notebook. In that way, you're out of it. Now get up. I'll make that couch into a bed and then call Barney."

"Why don't you have him pick you up here? That will keep him from suspecting that I'm here, and it'll keep you off the dark streets in the small hours."

"I'm not afraid of the dark, Dil."

"I didn't think I was, either."

When I came out of the small pink bathroom, the bed was made, a glass of water and two pills were on the coffee table, and Jill was just putting the phone back on the cradle.

"Take your drugs, Junior," she said. "Barney was pretty bitter about going back to work in the middle of the night, but he'll be right over."

She went into her bedroom to change. I slid under the

sheet in my underwear, took my pills, and turned out the
floor lamp at the end of the couch. She came out wearing
a tailored white suit, a big red purse slung over her
shoulder. She came to the couch.

"Going to be able to sleep, Dil?"

"Like dead."

She patted my cheek lightly. I caught her wrist, turned
her hand, and kissed her palm. She stood stock-still, her
hand trembling, before yanking it away. "Jack told you to
be good," she said.

Someone knocked at the wooden door at the end of the
entrance hall. " 'By now," she whispered. Her heels tick-
tocked down the hall. I heard the door open and a low
male voice. Then the door closed. I turned and looked out
through the glass into the court. The moon rode high
enough to slant into the court. The leering cupid had
acquired a silver highlight on its left cheek, shoulder, and
buttock. The tape around my middle felt like armor plate.
Sash weights hung on my eyelids. I tried to stay awake to
think of Laura, to re-evaluate Laura. I kept dropping into
blackness and then hauling myself back up to the edge of
consciousness by my fingernails. I do not remember the
last violent drop into a warm pool of sleep.

Coming awake was a slow process. The effect of the
sleeping pills was still with me. It was like being washed in
to shore. One wave would take me almost up onto the dry
beach, then suck me back out. Finally I landed, high, dry,
and awake. It was gray daylight. At first I thought it was
dawn. My watch said twelve. I listened to it. It was still
running. I had kicked the sheet off in the night. It was a
long painful process to get out of bed. Each individual
muscle had to do its share of groaning and screaming. My
joints cracked. There was a dull throb in my knuckles and
my ribs.

Jill's bedroom door was shut. I padded over to it and
put my ear flat against the panel. She wasn't snoring. She
was buzzing softly, like a bee full of honey. I went into
the bathroom. A face stared at me out of the mirror. One
eye was merely puffy. The other was puffy and purple.
The little bandage was white in contrast to a shipwreck

growth of whiskers. The tape around my middle precluded a shower. The pink tub was one of those squatty ones that sit catty-corner. I ran in about six inches of water as hot as I could stand it, and lowered myself in to both scrub and parboil. Shaving was more difficult. All I could find was a miniature gilt razor with an imitation jade handle. Perfumed bath soap had to double as shaving soap. The little razor not only cut a narrow furrow, it took every second hair out by the roots. Sandpaper would have been equally effective.

Nothing much could be done about my clothes. The alley fracas had aged them considerably. I dressed and went out into the court and looked up. The air felt like moist gray cotton. Low fat clouds scudded overhead.

Doing anything in a strange kitchen takes a lot of time. By the time I had her tray ready, with juice, toast, and coffee, I was hungry enough to eat the top off the electric stove. I took the tray to her bedroom door, shifted it to my left hand, turned the knob softly, and stuck my head in. I reacted like a turtle yanking his head back into his shell. I closed the door. By shutting the door, she had eliminated any hope of cross ventilation. Necessity had been the mother of ventilation. I swallowed hard and knocked on the door.

"Nguh, goway!" she mumbled.

"Breakfast, ma'am!"

"Whassat?"

"Breakfast."

"Minute. Jussa minute!"

I waited patiently until she said it was O.K. I went in. She was propped up in the double bed on two pillows. She had the pajamas back on, and the sheet was pulled up almost to her chin. The tray had little legs you could pop down with your thumbs. I set it across her lap. She didn't look radiant in the morning. She looked warm and tousled and sleepy and kitten-languid.

"Time, one o'clock. Weather, murky," I said.

She stared at me. "Good morning, waiter. I got in at seven. You snore."

"You make a weird buzzing sound."

95

Pink ran up her throat and exploded in her cheeks. "Did you look in and hear me?"

"I put my ear against the door."

She picked up the juice and the pink faded. "Oh," she said. She took a tentative sip. "Funny thing. I woke up with the horrid feeling that you'd been in here."

"I guess you dreamed it," I said. I backed toward the door. "My breakfast is out on the table. You know, I kind of resent the implication that I'd march into a lady's bedroom."

"I'm sorry, Dil."

"Psychopathic modesty. That's what you have."

"Probably. I said I was sorry."

I had reached the door. I grinned back at her. "Besides, if you ever have amnesia, they can prove who you are by that little crescent-shaped raspberry mark."

I thought she had blushed before. This one was so thorough that her face seemed to bulge. She made an incoherent sound and threw the empty juice glass at me. I reached out and caught it before it smashed against the wall by my head.

"When you're through with the coffee, throw the cup."

"Get out of here, damn you, Dillon Bryant!"

I was on my second cup of coffee when she stalked out of the bedroom and into the bathroom, clothes over her arm, nose in the air. She slammed the door. I finished the coffee, went in and got the tray, and washed the dishes before she came out. She wore a starched white blouse with short sleeves and ruffles at her throat and a tan tropical skirt.

"There's enough hot coffee for two more cups," I said. "Sit down."

She sat at the table with enormous dignity. I filled the clean cup. "Thank you," she said coldly.

"Funny how when you stare at a scene for no longer than one fifth of one second, a detail will stand out in your mind afterward."

"One fifth of one second?"

I shrugged. "Maybe even a tenth. Hell, I had the tray in my hand."

"And from the door? Not from in the room?"

96

"From the door. Feel better?"

"A little."

"I don't know why I'm humoring you, Miss Townsend. Any other gal of equal scenic value would be disappointed that I didn't come in and pull up a chair."

The blush was a little under control. "I can't help the way I am. I've always been that way. My God, the agonies I've gone through in shower rooms at college, in hospitals, in doctors' offices. When I go on the beach, I can just barely make myself leave the locker and walk out where the people are."

"Marriage ought to be quite a problem for you."

"I dread that part of it. Maybe then it will be all right."

"Enough of this clinical chatter. What happened last night?"

"I don't know whether Barney fell for it or not. He seemed to. But he's a very sharp little man. I don't think he asked enough questions about how you came to call me. He's annoyed at you, and even afraid for you, Dil. Every hour you stay out of touch strengthens Captain Paris' suspicions of you. The alley was pretty messy. Barney got hold of a cruiser and the men kept the people away while he went and got in touch with those federal people. That gave me my chance to nose around. Dil, did Siddman, the little man who killed him, search Haussmann's body?"

"He didn't touch it after it fell."

"Somebody did. They used a knife. All the pockets were slashed, and his clothes were cut away so that probably a money belt could be removed. And his shoes were gone."

"Some sneak thief that found him, you think?"

"I'd like to think that. But how about the shoes?"

"At one point I had his wallet in my hand."

"He'd been pretty brutally beaten about the face, Dil."

"I did all that. He trapped me when I followed him. He had some crazy woman with him that he took away from that messy business I told you about. I broke his knee and hit him with everything but one of the buildings, and he was still going strong enough to kill me with his hands when the fat man came along. Siddman, you said?"

"Barney identified him from the stuff in his pockets. He was a DP, and an expert leather worker. He lived alone. What happened to the woman?"

"I managed to knock Haussmann out long enough for her to get away. She left her mask behind."

"What sort of woman?"

"Well dressed. A certain look of breeding. But pretty sadly deranged in the sex department."

"I saw the mask. They'll try to trace it, you know. They think Siddman wore it. Anyway, the people Barney called arrived in force and took over. I was booted gently out of the area. I went down to the newsroom and wrote some fancy copy. Before I could turn it in, the night city editor had his orders. Haussmann became an 'unidentified man killed in a brawl.' And Siddman turns into just a routine heart-failure report. It's enough to drive an honest reporter nuts, frankly. But it's all wrapped up in a pretty package labeled 'Co-operation with the Authorities.'"

She took another sip of the coffee. "Say, you make good coffee!"

"That's a typical bachelor trait."

"Don't be so smug. The toast was burned."

"Carbon is good for you. But to get back. I don't like that search of Haussmann's body."

"Why not?"

"I don't think the body could have been found by accident. And that means that maybe there was a witness to the whole thing, somebody who stayed in the shadows and didn't much care who won. I came right here from the alley. I didn't even think of being followed. Damn it, Jill, I could have brought some unpleasant people to camp on your doorstep. I was careless. They could have tagged me back here, then gone back and stripped Haussmann of anything he was carrying. That business of the shoes, it sounds like what was done to Laura's shoes. Heels ripped off and soles peeled open. And that would mean that in addition to me and Siddman and the federal people, the ones who killed Laura were also hunting for Haussmann. It's a wonder that alley wasn't a mob scene out of De

Mille. It also means that they haven't found what they want yet."

As she started to speak, the sky opened like the bottom of a bucket and the roar of rain drowned her words. We scrambled around and closed the key windows.

Chapter Twelve

By FOUR O'CLOCK, when the sun came blearily through the thinning clouds to steam down on a sodden world, Jill had not yet returned from what she had called a "flying trip" to the newsroom to find out what was new.

I remembered how cute she had looked when she had turned to wave back at me as she went down the hall in her transparent rain cape, the hood covering her dark hair. I began to worry. Half a dozen times I went to the phone without lifting it from the cradle. Finally I dialed the *Star News* and asked for her.

"She was here for a while, but she left," the man said.

I did some more pacing. At a quarter to five I turned on the radio to catch the local news.

The sleek, greased voice of the local newscaster stopped the breath in my throat. "Warning to all citizens of New Orleans. This broadcast is being made at the request of police headquarters. Dillon Bryant, ex-employee of Trans-Americas Oil, is believed to be at large in the city. He has been charged with the murder of Elizabeth Morin, the shop clerk whose body was found in the apartment of another employee of Trans-Americas Oil. Fingerprints at the scene of the crime were compared with Bryant's prints in the files of Trans-Americas, and found to be identical. Samuel Spencer, head of the local office of Trans-Americas, admitted to the authorities that Bryant had demanded the key to the death apartment. A man answering Bryant's description was seen in the neighborhood of the apartment at the approximate time of the murder, and it is believed that Bryant may still have the apartment key in his possession.

"Early this morning a man was brutally murdered in an alley in the Quarter. He has not yet been identified. It was obvious that he put up a desperate fight. Two fingerprints of the assailant were obtained, one from the door of the room the murdered man had occupied under the name of Smith, the other from the lid of a trash can. The murdered man had been struck with the lid before being knifed. The fingerprints proved to have been made by Bryant. There is no known motive for the killing.

"Bryant is described as being six foot one, weight approximately one hundred and ninety pounds. Dark eyes, swarthy complexion. Black hair cut short. He is physically powerful and known to be dangerous. Please report the whereabouts of any man answering this description to the police at once. And now for other news in and around the city. The Mayor today announced that . . ."

I turned it off. If the radio carried it, the papers would carry it. And if I was found, Jill would have no excuse. None whatever. A large-size jam for Jill.

I couldn't imagine what the object was. Certainly Barney Zeck would know that I hadn't killed that girl. And the Jones boys would know. It was a trick of some sort. And I remembered spots on the front of Siddman's suit. His backward jump hadn't been quite fast enough. The knife would have his prints on it. I hadn't touched the knife.

There was an alternative idea. Suppose somebody wanted to tie the package up very neatly. I was one hell of a handy piece of string. Too bad they couldn't use me as the fall guy for Laura too.

The apartment began to turn into a sort of prison. Finally I phoned Tram Widdmar at his office. He was in.

"Tram? This is Dil."

"Jesus, man! Where are you?" he boomed. "Has everybody gone crazy all of a sudden? Or have you really turned killer? Where the hell are you?"

"Never mind that. You know Lieutenant Zeck, don't you?"

"Sure, I know Barney."

"Well, swing your weight around a little. Get hold of him. Make him tell you what kind of deal they're trying to rig on me. I'll phone you back later and get the story from you."

"If you show your face on the street, Dil, some trigger-happy character will probably shoot you down. Seen the papers? They got an old picture out of Sam's files and blew it up big."

"Oh, fine," I said bitterly.

"Boy, why don't you see if you can get out to the house? My people won't talk. And nobody will come around with any warrants. Besides, they already searched the place." His big laugh hurt my ear.

"It's an idea," I said.

"Hell, what are friends for, boy?"

"I'll let you know," I said. "I wouldn't want to try it until after dark, anyway."

A little after five I smoked my last cigarette. They never seem half as essential as they do after you run out. I prowled around, hunting for more. None in the kitchen or the living room. I tried the bedroom. I had yanked open the third bureau drawer, the lowest one, when suddenly I saw a half pack right in plain sight beside a box of powder on top of the bureau. I grabbed it and lit one. As I exhaled, I bent down to close the drawer. Under the edge of a sheer negligee, carefully folded, I saw the edge of a manila file folder. A typed title was pasted on the visible edge of the folder. It said, "Notes on Structure."

Structure of what? A thing like that can bother you. I'm a nosy type. And on minor matters, my conscience doesn't seem to operate. So I took out the folder. I sat on the bed and opened it. The notes were typed.

I   Bilateral structure indicated:
    A. Surface organization. Known sympathizers, Com-front organizations, student groups, pinks.
    B. Subsurface structure. Cellular structure; i.e., classic espionage. Ports, industrial centers—high priority. Personnel careful avoid any con-

tact with A above. Suspect consider people in A dupes. Most probably DPs, smuggled aliens. Adept sabotage, channeling of info. Probably many technical.

II Control mechanism (largely guesswork):

    A. One person, highly respected, in position to receive orders without suspicion and transmit to

    B. Co-ordinator of surface organization, who is less important than

    C. Co-ordinator of subsurface cellular organization.

III Summary of structure:

    A, above, is key. Must have money, power, mobility, access to communications. Must stay clear of any contact with surface organization, thus contact with surface co-ordinator must be cleverly handled. A—the man above suspicion—is keystone of arch. Essential to co-ordinated functioning.

There was more of it. A lot more of it. Enough so I began to understand why Jill showed no special shock when I mentioned who the "Morin" girl had worked for. I remembered Jill's remarkable work in ferreting out the smuggling game. I knew what I held in my hand. It was her own private project. Heaven only knew the working hours that had gone into it.

On the last page I found a note. A short note. It was in the form of a question. "Is Dil marrying subsurface operative? Believe too flamboyant. Uses mostly little gray people. Laura anything but gray. Turncoat? Possibly. Then party dangerous."

The last three words meant almost nothing. The party was dangerous. Well, the party had proved dangerous to Laura. They had sent an operative after her and the operative had killed her. How dangerous can the party get?

I put the folder back in the drawer, careful to replace it as it was. And now I had even better cause for worry. Jill was messing with clever people. The odds were against anyone's being able to investigate without that investigation's being sensed, and resented. If "they" had seen me come to Jill from that bloody alley, and if they had become conscious that Jill's tilted nose was aimed at their affairs, then they might add two and two, get seven, and do something about it. Something drastic.

At a few minutes past six the door opened. I went down the hall at a run and caught her by both arms as she shut the door behind her. I shook her and she dropped her cape.

"Dil! What on earth?"

"Flying trip, eh? Great flying trip!"

"For goodness' sake, stop growling at me. And stop hurting my arms."

I released her and picked up the cape. "You could have phoned," I said haughtily.

"I thought of it, and then decided you were too smart to answer if it did ring."

"That argument has a little merit, maybe."

She stamped her foot. "You're beginning to make me feel like a high-school girl who stayed out too late."

We walked toward the living room. "I was worried. Very worried," I said.

She gave me an oblique look. "You should be worried." She handed me the *Star News,* a Sunday extra, a very rare item. I opened it up. The guy on the front page looked like a criminal. Me.

I sat down with the paper. Essentially it was the same as what had come over the radio, with the addition of a few unpretty details about both murders, and a generous hint that I was a homicidal maniac.

She took two new packs of cigarettes out of her purse and put them on the coffee table. "I had a chat with Barney, Dil."

I threw the paper aside. "That'll save me calling Tram back."

"You phoned Tram? Did you tell him where you were?"

"No. I half promised I'd be his house guest. I better take the heat off you. Can you drive me out there after dark?"

"I left the car in front. But you're safe here, Dil. Really you are."

"Even from Barney? What did he say?"

103

"He was odd. Very subdued. He gave me some hard looks out of those pale eyes of his. He said that if you, by any chance, should show up here, I better shoo you away fast. So I grinned at him and asked him how he could be so certain you weren't here already. It seemed like a good remark to make at the time."

"How did he take it?"

"He smiled back. A weak smile, sort of. He said that for the sake of my reputation, I better chase you out. He baffled me. I had the feeling he wanted to tell me more, but had promised not to, or something. Look, Dil. Tell me one thing. The truth and nothing but the truth. Did Laura give you anything to keep for her?"

"Nothing."

"Did she give you any presents?"

"There wasn't much time for that. Oh, here. This little rabbit. She made me wait on the sidewalk while she went into a jewelry shop, that big one near the corner of Iberville and Dauphine, and bought this rabbit for me."

Jill took it casually, looked at it, and handed it back. "No, that doesn't fit," she sighed. "Oh, damn! I wish this all made more sense. I think it would probably be all right if you went out and stayed with Tram. It isn't really necessary, though."

"You mean you *can* lock that bedroom door?"

"You have a nasty knack of making me blush like a fool. There's no key to that lock, or it would have been locked last night."

She changed from her heat-wilted clothes while I made drinks. She got back into the blue linen sun suit. We sat and an awkward silence grew between us. I glanced at her. She was looking out across the small court.

"It's some kind of trick I don't understand," I said.

"Charging you with the murders?"

"Of course. But you're better able to understand it than I am."

"How do you mean?"

"You and your careful research. Adding two and two."

She stared at me. "You sound a little contemptuous,

Dil. As though there were something nasty about the sort of prying I do."

"I didn't mean to sound that way. You know, Jill, I've never told you this before, but I've always felt a little awed by you. You've always seemed so controlled, so self-contained. You know, I never saw you off base before, like when I brought you your breakfast."

"How perfectly absurd! Goodness, I never feel self-contained. I'm always rattled about something, or afraid of something. I never seem to make the right impression on people—the impression I want to make."

"Then you've got one hell of a good act, Jill."

"Better than I knew," she said softly. "Refill?"

I held out the empty glass. She didn't meet my eyes as she took it. She carefully avoided touching my hand. As she walked away, I said, "And that yak about bathing suits. Did it mean anything? You spend a lot of time in a sun suit."

She turned and stared back at me, and I could sense the anger that stirred in her. "I do things because they're difficult, Dil. I do things I don't like to do as a form of self-discipline."

"Does having me here come under that heading?"

"You make me so darn mad! You twist everything around, in that superior way of yours. And inside you're laughing at me."

"With you, my lamb. Not at you."

The larder was low. I helped her inspect the cupboards. The meal we had was abundant enough, but a slightly odd assortment. After the dishes were done we sat in silence and watched night obscure the bronze boy. There was a smell of new rain in the air, and the stars came out only to wink for a few moments in the early night sky before the clouds covered them.

"Any time now," I said.

I saw the pale outline of her face turn toward me. "At least you don't have to pack, do you?"

"Tram will have some things that will fit. These clothes feel like I'll have to take them off with a trowel."

"I won't go in with you, so there's no point in changing, I guess. I'm ready when you are."

She turned on the floor lamp at the head of the couch and picked up her purse, and we went down the hallway to the wooden door that fronted on the sidewalk.

"I'm forever grateful to you, Jill," I said softly.

"Don't make such a thing out of it. When I kill my managing editor, you can hide me in your pocket."

She had her hand on the door latch. The light from the living room was faint. I took her wrist and pulled her hand away from the latch, turning her toward me. Her whole body stiffened. I slid my hand down around her fingers. They felt like ice. I put my other hand on her shoulder, and knew that she trembled. It was the clumsiest possible kiss, with our noses getting in the way, and her lips tightly compressed under mine. I realized what a mistake it was to make any attempt to step out of the brotherly role. She made me feel as if I were all hands and feet.

"Sorry," I said.

"I guess I'm no good, Dil. I'm not often kissed."

"I hope the next guy does a better job than that, anyway. Come on. Let's roll."

After two blocks I said, "Hey! Wouldn't it be a little embarrassing to be picked up?"

She didn't answer me. She sat on a seat cushion that kept her high enough so that she could lean forward and grasp the top of the wheel of the battered coupé. Somebody kept the motor in sweet shape for her. She gunned it up to each corner, took a quick stab at the brake, and wrenched hard, letting the wheel slip back through her hands as the coupé swayed back into line.

I had to force myself to lean back and relax. She looked straight ahead and her lips were a firm, tight line. She barged across Canal, got on Tulane near Charity Hospital, and roared out Tulane, weaving through traffic, to the Airline Highway. The motor began to sing like a big bee.

"Damn it, Jill, take it easy!"

She didn't answer me. She just depressed the foot throttle another fraction of an inch. She took the cutoff to Metairie Road and skidded the back wheels as she took the oblique onto Metairie. When we reached Tram's, she waited until the last instant before braking and ducking into his drive. A few house lights were on.

"Here you are," she said coldly.

That's as far as I got. She left me looking at the twin red tail lights as she spun away. She left me rubbing my elbow where the window frame had rapped it smartly, wondering what was wrong with her.

Sammy opened the door a few moments after I leaned on the bell. He peered out at me and his eyes grew wide and he took an involuntary half step backward. Then he pulled himself together and said, "Evening, Mr. Bryant Come in, suh. Mr. Widdmar, he's out in the patio, suh."

"Thanks, Sammy." I went through onto the central patio. Tram was a bulky shadow enfolded in a Barwa chair. Lights in the house proper picked up glints from the glassware on the tray table at his elbow

"The condemned man ate a hearty Scotch," I said.

"Mix your own, you felon," Tram boomed. Sammy brought a second chair out and set it down with a soft scrape of aluminum on the patio tiles I made my drink and sat down, feeling at ease for the first time in many days.

"Hope I'm not intruding," I said.

"I've been sitting out here crying into the night. I had a nice tasty setup for this evening. Tall and demure and cautious and widowed and potentially hotter than Mammy's pressure cooker. I had mood music all stacked on the machine. A duck-and-wild-rice dinner, with brandy to float on top of it. What do you think I built this house for? As a refuge for fugitives from justice, or as an adjunct to seduction?"

"What did you tell her?"

"That I had to sit up with a sick friend. Feeble, wasn't it?"

"Nothing like making me feel at home, Tram."

"Es su casa, as we old bullfighters say. Barney was enigmatic. Where the hell were you hiding?"

"Under a wet rock."

"So? You know, I thought I heard the loose connecting rods on Jill's heap just before you arrived. Sound carries nice on this night air. And I decided that Jill's place would have made a nice little hidey-hole for you, even though the young lady is colder than the proverbial well-digger's wallet."

"From experience you speak?"

"From the experience of futile attempts, during which I was laughed at. Hideous thing for a man of my sensibilities. Always thought there was hidden talent there. Did she make you comfy?"

"On the couch."

He turned and awkwardly fixed a new drink. His brown chest was bare and he wore the perennial faded sarong. There is a wide band of rubbery fat around his middle. Not unhealthy fat. Rather, the sort of fat you see on middle-aged Hawaiians who still do a lot of swimming and fishing.

"To descend into pure corn for a moment, Dil, let me say that I am your boy. Lawyers, pressure, refuge, or alley-type fisticuffs."

I felt a stinging sensation in my eyes. A friend is a rare thing, and precious. "Thanks, Tram."

"There will now be a brief interlude of music, mostly violins."

"Tram, I'm being pushed around without entirely knowing why."

"That sounds revoltingly familiar. What does it remind me of? Ah, yes. Our Army careers. Hurry up and wait, soldier."

I'd been a battalion commander of an engineer outfit on Pick's Pike, more commonly known as the Ledo Road. Or the Stilwell Road. My outfit pushed the lead cats out along the track. Tram had been on the staff at Ledo Headquarters, Advance Section I. We'd had a few laughs, a few monumental drunks at Calcutta, a pair of cute little No'th Ca'lina nurses from the station hospital at Chabua. We'd been shot at in anger, and we'd hated the same general officers, and we'd lived through a couple of monsoon seasons while atabrine turned us as yellow as the Chinese troops heading down the line to Myitkyina.

Nobody had saved anybody's life. We'd just got along pretty well. Assam and North Burma hadn't sapped Tram's energy or lessened his bounce. We'd agreed to keep in touch after the war. We might not have done that had I not worked out of the New Orleans office of Trans-Americas, his home town and great love.

"That was a hell of a mess, the way Laura was killed, Dil."

"It was pretty cold and pretty professional."

"When you have something that somebody wants badly enough to kill you for, then you better get rid of it. You know, I've been thinking and thinking about it. I've talked with Bill French. We've been wondering what the hell it was she smuggled in. What do you think it was, Dil? Jewels? Dope?"

"Information. Some kind of document. Spy stuff, Tram." With what he was doing for me, it would have been pretty stuffy to clam up on him.

"Shades of Mr. Oppenheim, eh? Plans of the secret weapon. Cloaks and daggers under a waning moon."

"I know how it must sound to you. It sounded that way to me, too. Now I'm used to it. Hell, as far as I'm concerned now, there's a spy behind every bush."

"O.K. Even though it's intellectually painful, I'll go along with the assumption that she brought in some kind of information. Did they get it from her?"

"No. She got rid of it somehow. Or maybe it was memorized."

"But I don't suppose they could take a chance that it was memorized—that is, if it was highly important?"

"No. She had a partner. Maybe he had it. He's dead. Maybe they took it off him. If so, then the heat will be off me. The damn fools still think I've got it."

"And you haven't?"

"Hell, no!"

He was silent for a while. He said, "Dil, I know you pretty well. I know just how stubborn you can be. It would be just like you to hang onto something she gave you just out of pure orneriness."

"Brother, if I had it, I wouldn't have it any longer. I would have given it to the right people and they'd have it in Washington by now, believe me."

"Parlor patriot?"

"Call it that if you want to."

"You'd turn it in, even when it might lead you to the

guy who killed Laura if you should hang onto it?"

I gave my answer considerable thought. When I spoke my voice sounded far away, and very tired. "A funny thing, Tram. I was panting around wanting to get my hands on the guy who killed her. I wanted to kill him with my hands. But I've learned a lot of things. And now I don't care too much any more. I think maybe Laura was overdue for killing. I think she had done some things that canceled out her right to keep living. I almost hope she died hard. She was just a disease I had for a while. I can look back on my time with her the way you look back on a fever, a high fever that blurs outlines and intensifies colors."

"Pliers and a wire coat hanger don't make what you'd call a very merciful weapon, Dil."

"I think she was unconscious when it was done. I feel a hell of a lot sorrier for that little girl I'm supposed to have killed in Harrigan's apartment. She knew what was coming, and just how it was going to be done."

"Are you sorry for the big guy in the alley, too?"

"Not exactly." It was bone-weariness, I guess, but the two drinks plus what I'd had at Jill's made my lips feel thick and numb. I felt a little dizzy too. I heard myself talking about Haussmann, about Talya, about all manner of things.

"Get it all off your chest, boy," Tram said softly. "Talk it out. That's the best way. I'll fix you another."

The words poured out. A monotonous flood. It was good of Tram to sit and listen to it all.

I gabbled like a girl. The cornflowers for Talya. The guy with the sunburned nose, cleaning his fingernails. Jill's research file. The color of Siddman's face. As I talked, my voice slowly went rusty, and my lips wouldn't fit around the words any more.

Vaguely I can remember leaning heavily on Tram as he walked me into the bedroom. I can remember staring into a bathroom mirror at a face that didn't look like mine, then falling across the bed.

When I awakened Monday morning it was ten o'clock and Tram had gone to his office. I've never felt worse.

Sammy brought in some clothes of Tram's. They bagged around the middle, but they were clean.

My stomach quivered on the edge of nausea. It was a full hour before I could attempt black coffee, liberally laced with brandy. It was Sammy's polite recommendation. It worked fine. At about eleven-thirty I had a genuine breakfast and read the morning paper. I was still the object of a city-wide man hunt. It was like reading about somebody else. I remembered the way Jill had acted when she drove me out the night before, and I began to wonder what I could do. I was dialing when Sammy came silently up behind me and reached around me and pushed the cradle buttons down.

"Terrible sorry, suh, but Mr. Widdmar, he left strict orders for you to do no telephonin' today."

I shrugged. It was probably a pretty smart idea. Tram stood to lose a lot if anyone got a line on where I was hiding. I played some of his old jazz records, took a swim, and managed to get thoroughly restless.

Chapter Thirteen

TRAM came bouncing lustily in a little after five, shedding his city clothes, singing in a thunderous baritone about a lady known as Lou. He came out in flowered trunks and plunged, snorting and bellowing, into the pool.

It wasn't until he came out onto the poolside mattress, puffing and hammering water out of his ear, that I got a chance to talk to him.

"Have a good day?" he said.

"Oh, dandy! Any more days like this and you better send your demure damosel around before boredom drives me nuts."

"I thought you'd be too busy with your hangover."

"It really hit me last night."

"Your energy was down, I think."

JOHN D. MACDONALD

"I'm glad you didn't make a recording of that gab fest, Tram."

"I let you talk, and it was a struggle. I'd rather hear myself talk any time."

"Look, I've got to decide what to do. It's a nice house and all that, but I can't spend the rest of my life here."

"I've been thinking about that, too. Dil, I don't think you ought to risk bucking the officials on this. They grab you and they're going to have a time. I made some calls. This hiding hasn't done you any good. I've been kidding around, Dil, but right now I'm serious. I think you ought to get the hell out of town. Maybe out of the country, and let this thing blow over."

"You're kidding!"

"I'm not. That's the bad part of it. You don't know what public hysteria can do. They're about to hang you in effigy down there in the city. And let me ask you one question. Can you prove, Dil, beyond the shadow of a doubt, that you *didn't* kill that girl and the guy in the alley?"

"No, but—"

"You'd have to have that sort of proof to make it a good gamble to turn yourself in. You know I don't get hysterical. But right now I'm actually afraid of what they might do to you if they get their hands on you."

"This sounds crazy!"

"Boy, how many men have been strapped into the chair or dropped through the trap thinking, They can't do this to me? Use your head."

"What have you got in mind?"

"I've got the contacts. It shouldn't be too much of a trick to send you down the river on a freighter. Venezuela might be all right. You know your way around in Venezuela."

"Somehow, it doesn't seem like a good idea. I'm going to have to think about it, Tram. Even so, I don't think I'll do it."

"You better do something."

"That's for sure. Look, I want to get in touch with Jill."

"I don't think that's so smart."

"Hell, Tram. She knows I'm here."

112

"I don't think you should."

"Look. Thanks a hell of a lot for the refuge and all that. But let me decide who I get in touch with. Getting hold of Jill won't get you in a jam."

"Suppose my phone is tapped? What then?"

"Get hold of her yourself. Ask her to come on out here. She's smart enough not to give anything away on the phone."

"What good will it do to talk to her?"

"That's what I mean, Tram. Let me decide that."

"What are you getting all heated up about?"

"I'm not heated up. This place is fine until it begins to smell like a jail."

"You don't understand the risk I'm taking. They might even jail me for hiding you here."

I took a deep breath. There was a faintly surly look on his broad cupid's face. "Tram. Listen to me. I want to talk to Jill. The why of it is none of your business. Let me phone her, or you phone her to come out here."

"Is that some kind of ultimatum?"

"The alternative is that I go in and see her."

"They'll pick you up, sure."

"I'll take that chance."

He braced himself on one elbow and gave me a slow lewd grin. "She must be hotter than I thought, boy."

My own reaction surprised and shocked me. It was totally unexpected. One minute he was grinning up at me and the next instant I had kicked him off the rubberized mattress into his own pool. I wanted to cut my foot off at the ankle.

He floundered up over the edge and stared at me. "What the hell, Dil?"

"I'm sorry. I didn't mean to do that. I don't know why I did it. Believe me."

He inspected the abrasion on his brown chest. He seemed more shocked than angry. Then, surprisingly, he began to laugh. He laughed so hard he fell down and rolled on the mattress and the tears rolled out of his eyes.

"All right," he said, when he could get his breath. "I'll phone the black-haired wench for you." He grabbed my

113

wrist and looked at my watch. "Probably won't get her, but I'll try."

"What makes you think you won't get her?"

"Oh, there's a party I think she was invited to. We'll try."

He padded into the house, leaving damp footprints. I was on his heels. He found the number on his phone pad and dialed. I stood close enough to him so that I could hear it ringing in her apartment. It rang three times.

He took the phone from his ear and smiled at me. "See? You'll have to—"

I heard an odd sound come over the wire. I snatched the phone out of his hand. There was a thudding sound and a faint weak cry. And the phone in her apartment was carefully replaced.

"She's in trouble!" I shouted at Tram. "Let's get down there!"

His eyes were wide and round. "God! Look in the front of the book. Give me the police number. They can get there faster than we can."

"Dial the operator."

He did so. He stood close to the table. I jittered with impatience. Then he said, "Sergeant? I just phoned Miss Jill Townsend and heard sounds of a struggle, some sort of trouble at her apartment, I think." I heard him give the address as I paced nervously back and forth.

There was a mirror at the corner of the hallway. Tram's back was to me. I happened to glance in the mirror. I saw that he held the phone in his right hand. The thick index finger of his left hand was holding the cradle down. He was talking into a dead line. I looked at his broad, brown wet back and felt a sudden sense of shock and horror stronger even than what I felt in that instant when I saw Talya's body.

"And I'll phone back in a while and find out, Sergeant," he said.

It gave me just time to collect myself, to forcibly restrain myself from spinning him around and smashing him in the mouth. My face wasn't under control yet. As he hung up, I turned away and walked blindly out toward the patio. He padded along behind me and put his hand on my shoulder and said soothingly, "That's the best way, boy. They'll radio a cruiser. It's probably heading for her place right now."

"What do you think it could be?" I asked, keeping my voice as steady as I could.

"God only knows. Maybe it was just a touch of heat exhaustion. She might have fainted just as she picked up the phone or something."

I had enough control then to turn around and look at him. His smile was broad and pleasant. My good friend Tram. My buddy.

"Say!" he said. "I better get dressed."

"I'll come along and keep you entertained with light conversation."

"You do that."

I hadn't been in his bedroom before. It was the most enormous bed I had ever seen. At least ten feet long and eight feet wide.

"How do you like my skating rink, boy?"

"Very, very fancy."

He eeled out of the swimming trunks and went into the big bathroom. The shower stall had a glass door. I let him get in and get his head soaped. I took a jar of deodorant from the shelf over the sink and wrapped it in a towel. His back was to the glass door. I yanked it open and swung the towel like a sap. The padded glass chunked against his skull. He swayed, tried to turn, and went down in a flaccid heap. I turned off the shower and dragged him out into the center of the bathroom floor.

I knotted neckties tightly around his wrists and ankles. There was tape in the cabinet. I shoved two more ties into his mouth and crisscrossed the tape across his lips. He was heavy and slippery, but I got him on my shoulder and staggered in and dropped him on the bed. I yanked both sheets from under him, soaked one in the shower, and wrapped it tightly around him. I turned him face down and covered him with the second sheet. Then I found the drapery cords and darkened the room. He had emptied his pockets onto the top of the bureau. I took his car keys, looked at the dwindling state of my own finances, and emptied his wallet into mine.

As I shut the bedroom door quietly behind me, Sammy was coming down the hall. I held my finger to my lips. "He's got a hell of a headache, Sammy. He's trying to take a nap. He told me to tell you. If he can get to sleep, he doesn't want to be awakened for dinner."

"Not like him, suh," Sammy said, frowning. "He never feels poorly."

"He does today. I've got an errand in town. I'm borrowing a car. That Ford will be O.K."

"I'll bring it around, suh. And you be careful you don't get caught, Mr. Bryant."

"I'll be careful."

Every foot of the way back to the Quarter I felt as though thousands of eyes were watching me. I circled Jill's block on Ursulines. Pedestrian traffic seemed normal. There was no sign of her car. I couldn't see it in the tiny parking lot where she usually leaves it when it isn't parked in front of her door. I was glad I had forgotten to return her key, and that she had forgotten to ask for it. I parked, got the key in my hand, and walked as casually as I could up to the wooden door. I inserted the key gently, careful to keep out of line of the tiny view hole cut in the door. The lock clicked open. I yanked the door open and went in fast, pulling it shut behind me. I flattened myself against the wall and listened. I could hear the slow drip of a faucet, nothing else.

My heart was hammering and blood was roaring in my ears as I inched forward.

The apartment was empty. A chair had been moved close to the grillework iron door, on the living-room side of it. Two nylon stockings lay knotted and slashed on the floor, one still looping the chair leg. It wasn't hard to reconstruct what had happened.

Jill had been there, tied to the chair. The phone had rung. Those who guarded her had intended that it should ring unanswered. But the phone was on the other side of the grillework door from the chair. Probably a loop of the wire had sagged through the bars of the door. Somehow Jill had managed to yank on the wire and pull the phone off, had tried to scream for help.

Those who guarded her had no way of knowing who

had heard the cry. So they had immediately cut her loose and taken her away. I went into the bedroom. The folder was gone. I looked carefully around the area of the chair. Near the door, on the floor, I found two spots of blood, each one no bigger than a dime. They were still wet and fresh. It made me feel as though someone had stabbed me in the belly with a broad-bladed knife, turning it with the thrust.

What the hell did they want with her?

The Jills of this world should be kept out of this sort of mess.

I went back down the hallway and looked through the small hole cut through the door. Some scrawny female young fry were skipping a languid rope across the street. A young girl leaned crossed tan forearms on the shaded window sill facing the banquette and talked earnestly to a sultry-looking young man who leaned against the wall beside the window, his face a mask of arrogant boredom. A sway-backed horse clopped slowly down the street, pulling a trash wagon, his sagging skin rippling under the flies.

My range of vision was restricted. Across the street I could see a sharp black shadow of a man. I could not see the man who cast the shadow. He leaned against a post. His hat was tilted back off his forehead. He did not move. I weighed my chances. Maybe he was watching the doorway. Maybe he had seen me go in. Maybe he was a guy killing time, or waiting for a girl. Soon the sun would go beyond the cornice of the building, and I would be able to see his shadow no longer. The clothes Tram had lent me were not exactly what you'd call inconspicuous. The white linen trousers were so baggy at the waist that I wore the shirt outside of them. The short-sleeved shirt was pallid green, with dark blue sailfish leaping on it.

It was twenty steps to the car. Probably just a guy waiting for somebody else. Dangerous to stay here too long.

And then his shadow changed. I saw the arms come up, the head dip. It was an odd, suggestive pattern. I thought for a moment he was winding a watch. His right wrist kept turning slowly. And suddenly I realized that he was cleaning his fingernails. And I knew who he was. I knew Laura had seen him. And Jill. And Talya.

I heard a twanging voice coming up the sidewalk on my side, heard the shuffle of many feet. "Now, ladies and gentlemen, ahead on your left you will see the old Ursulines Convent. The Ursulines of France were the Gray Sisters. They made a contract to educate the young-uns here in Louisiana, and the first of them came over here in 1726. You will notice the architecture, particularly the . . ."

At the moment when the group was directly opposite the door, I slipped out quickly. I hoped to go along with the group for a few paces, and get into the car quickly enough to get away. I bumped into a stocky perspiring woman who had gloves in one hand and a stringy daughter in the other. She glared at me. I apologized meekly. There were about twenty people in the group, about five of them men. The guide was a withered little man with a peaked motorman's hat and a penetrating voice. The tourists looked as if they had been trudging around for far too long.

I glanced quickly toward the other curb, toward the post. He was as Jill had described him. A sandy man with a tight, give-nothing face. He wore a pale gray suit, well-pressed, and a brown cocoa straw hat with a maroon band. Late twenties, I guessed—perhaps older. Our eyes met in that instant. He held the match with which he had been cleaning his nails. He was motionless, his elbows out-thrust slightly. There was no look of surprise on his face, just a watchfulness. Then with a deft muscular daintiness, somewhat reminiscent of Cagney in moments of anticipated brutality, he tossed the match back over his shoulder and started across the street. I could see him out of the corner of my eye. I began to shoulder my way forward through the slow-moving group.

"The Gray Sisters had a lot of trouble, folks. The ship they came over on hit a rock and nearly sank. They were becalmed. Pirates nearly got them. They got stuck on a sand bar out in the Gulf. All in all, it took them five dreadful months to make the trip from France to the mouth of the river, and another week to come upriver to New Orleans by canoe."

I reached the car, and just as I grasped the door handle the man opened the door on the far side of the car and slid behind the wheel. I let go of the door handle and kept on with the group. Twenty paces further on I glanced back. He had left the car and was sauntering along behind us.

"This is all so terribly interesting," a gaunt woman said at my elbow.

"It certainly is," I said. She glared at me. She had been speaking to a plump young girl trodding wearily along behind her.

"In those days New Orleans was a pretty fearful place for the Gray Sisters to come to. Imagine it. Damp and miserable. Just a bunch of shacks. Floods coming in over the levees all the time. Alligators bellering at night."

I looked back again. The man had casually made himself a part of the group. The guide stopped on the corner. He stared at me. "Fella, are you joining this here tour?"

"If you don't mind," I said.

"You missed most of it, but it will still cost you two dollars."

"I'll pay for both of us," a soft, controlled voice said at my elbow. Straw Hat handed over four dollars. He was so close to me I could see a streak of blond stubble on his cheek, stubble that the razor had missed.

The guide took the money and gave us a dubious look. He moved off through the gathering shadows of early evening, the party following him.

The man came up beside me. "This is no good, you know."

"I always wanted to take one of these tours."

"You kill me, Bryant." Yes, Talya had said that he had made himself very American.

"Now, this is Gallatin Street, folks. Once upon a time it was a pretty gay kind of street. Man could get himself knifed here with no trouble at all. Used to be headquarters for the Mafia gangs, this little street did. In '34, I think it was, they took away part to make room for the new French Market. That's it over there. Anybody feel like buying any snails today?"

119

The group cackled obediently.

"This isn't doing Miss Townsend any good, Bryant."

"You've got the whip hand. All you've got to do is yell cop. What do you want from me?"

"That can be explained better in private. I just want to talk to you. Let's go back to your car."

"How did you know I was coming?"

"I didn't. I just wanted to see who had phoned her. She was very clever and very foolish and very brave. Having you come was a bit of luck, now."

"Can't you fellas be quiet back there so people can hear?" the guide complained.

I stopped. We were at the corner of Gallatin and Governor Nicholls Streets. The tour went on down Governor Nicholls Street toward the Haunted House. I put my back against a building.

"We'll talk here." I debated my chances of taking a quick swing at him.

He had all the extra senses of a jungle animal. He moved away, glanced in both directions, then let his coat fall open just enough so that I could see the gleaming butt plate of the holstered automatic.

"I could give it to you on the street and win myself a medal," he half whispered.

"You have something to say, I believe."

"We found out that Miss Townsend was taking an unhealthy interest in some of the organizational aspects of our group, Bryant. We were curious about what you two may have talked about. As you know from the stupid girl who thought she could double-cross us, we're still after a certain document. We're not convinced that it doesn't exist here in this city. Until we find it, no risk is too great to take. I must emphasize that."

"You haven't said anything yet."

"I saw you start to search Haussmann's body, Bryant. You handled yourself very well, by the way. It left me with a pretty problem when the stranger showed up. I didn't know whether to step in and save you or not."

"Siddman saved you the trouble."

"Very emotional man, apparently, that Siddman. It was nice to find you again, the other night. I followed you to

Miss Townsend's place, and then went back and searched Haussmann's body. A necessary risk. He didn't have it. I know it isn't on your person. But, Bryant, I do know that you know where it is."

"I don't."

"Please don't waste time, Bryant." He paused until a stroller was out of earshot. "We had one of our people phone Miss Townsend. His voice is not unlike yours. For one moment Miss Townsend was fooled. I will repeat her exact words. She said, 'Dil, that document they want is— Let me hear your voice again, Dil.' As we had phoned from the neighborhood, we were able to arrive just as she came out the door. Now you see my point. Miss Townsend is a surprisingly stubborn young woman. Both of you share the information we want. Surely you don't want us to test the extent of her bravery and her determination, Bryant."

"What are you getting at?"

"Just that some people can be persuaded with very little bodily harm. I am afraid Miss Townsend is not one of those. The proper drugs, the ones used in the mother country, are not available here. We are banking on your personal regard for the girl."

"Have you hurt her?" I asked. My voice sounded thick.

"Just a little. Just enough to discover the extent of her stubbornness."

"But you can get the information from her?"

"Of course. Everyone has a breaking point. It takes time. We've already taken too much time."

It had been on the tip of my tongue to say that Jill had been going to tell me something about the document that I didn't know. The danger was that I might have convinced him. And then he would have shaken me off and gone back to Jill. I was in no position to hunt for her. The day grew darker by the moment. Straw Hat glanced up at the sky. The black clouds were rolling across the city, obscuring the sunset.

"What kind of deal can I make?" I asked him.

"Can you produce the document?"

"Maybe. If Jill is turned loose at once. If I'm cleared

121

of suspicion regarding Haussmann and the Dvalianova girl."

"Those things can be discussed after we have the document and after we've inspected it to see if it's genuine."

"I'm supposed to trust you?"

"Why not? You don't have much choice, do you?" He seemed completely at ease. He rocked back and forth from his heels to the balls of his feet.

"I don't think you're as confident as you look."

He stopped rocking. "That's an odd thing to say."

"How about this. Maybe this will shake you a little. The Townsend girl does not know where the document is. I asked her to find out exactly what it is. That's what she started to tell me, to tell the man who sounded like me. But she doesn't know where it is."

I've played a lot of poker. You can't run a bluff too bravely. It makes it look like a bluff. You can't underplay it without achieving the same result. There is a narrow area between extreme confidence and faint uncertainty where a bluff has a chance of succeeding.

The faint look of dismay in his eyes was immediately concealed. I followed it up quickly. "As far as the girl is concerned, she means exactly nothing to me. I was sticking with her because in a spot like I'm in, it's nice to have a newspaper on your side. You can do what you damn please with her. Ethically, I want to make her part of any bargain I make with you. But to me the other considerations are more important. Plus a certain amount of cash."

"I can't authorize a cash payment."

"You can check with someone who can, though."

"Possibly, Bryant."

"Where is the girl?"

"In a safe place."

He glanced down the street. At that moment he was within range. I could have taken that moment to slam my fist against the unprotected angle of his jaw. Nothing would have been gained. I was beginning to understand him better. A classic word fitted him. Hireling. Like a wind-up toy that will go dutifully in the intended direction. Now the wind-up toy had run into the leg of a chair. The wheels still turned. But it had to be picked up, rewound, and headed in the new direction.

"You won't take my word," he said.

"Not for anything. I wouldn't take your word that in another half hour it's going to be dark."

"All we want is the document. Nothing else."

"This is a stalemate, isn't it?"

He shifted uneasily. "It can be worked out."

"Not standing here on the corner, my friend."

He made up his mind. "You can wait at the girl's apartment. I'll tell them what you want."

"Understand, I'd rather be picked up by the police than have you people get hold of me. Maybe I'd talk quicker than the girl."

He gave me a long look. "It is possible. Somehow I don't think so."

"And maybe," I said, "I've arranged things so that if I'm out of touch for too long, a friend will turn the document over to the Washington people."

He licked his lips. "They're all over the city. They've made things more difficult than we'd thought."

"I don't want to go to the girl's apartment. I'll wait in the car I came in."

"It will take maybe a half hour."

I took a deep breath. We started to walk, side by side. Friends strolling casually through the blue city. I seemed to see us as though I were a third person looking down onto the street. A big guy in a fancy shirt taking long strides. A smaller man, carefully dressed, walking with that oddly delicate muscular precision. A hunted man and a subversive agent, looking like a pair of tourists heading for the bright lights.

Chapter Fourteen

On the way back to the car I tried to think of some course of action. I knew that I wasn't adept enough to follow Straw Hat. And very probably he would go directly to a phone. And very possibly he would phone the Metairie Road home of one Tram Widdmar. I couldn't figure it any other way.

I kept remembering Jill's fragmentary notes on structure. There had to be an A. Mr. A would be top coordinator for both the surface and subsurface groups. There was a clear, clean line of deduction that made Tram appear as Mr. A. He had money, power, influence, freedom, access to communications, access to port traffic. If he prevented the police from knowing of Jill's difficulty by keeping his finger on the phone cradle, it could only mean that he had prior knowledge that she was in difficulty. His reluctance to have me attempt to get in touch with her was a tip-off to that effect. Her difficulties had to spring directly from what I had told him. I had told him that I had stayed with her. I had told him of the folder. I had talked too damn much. That talking jag was odd. Not typical. And the brutal hangover the next morning was indicative. It suddenly appeared obvious that something had been added to my drinks. Some drug that would have the effect of loosening the tongue. Scopolamine, or something of that nature.

The next deductive step was frighteningly clear. My attack on Tram would indicate to him that somehow I had found out. That made me dangerous to him. If I were picked up by the police, he might be through. Maybe he couldn't stand the sort of investigation that would result. To protect his cover, I had to be eliminated. If the man walking at my side were to get in touch with Tram, the mechanical toy would be set in motion, aimed at me.

Better that the hireling be eliminated than the keystone of the arch fall.

I thought of the Tram I had known. I saw him in a new way. That booming, bouncing exterior seemed more false the more I thought of it. It was window dressing. Good old Tram. Party boy. Bland-faced brown cupid. But native-born. How had they got to Tram? How had they made him believe? Did he fancy himself as the future commissar of New Orleans? I wondered if I should have struck harder. Removing Tram suddenly seemed more important than anything that could happen to Jill or myself. I knew, without any shadow of doubt, that Jill would feel the same.

We reached the car. Straw Hat said, "You stay right here. It's dark enough now so that there isn't much chance of anyone recognizing you." He walked briskly to the corner. I waited a full two minutes and then let myself back into the apartment.

I phoned Sam Spencer. The man who takes care of him answered and connected me immediately with Sam.

"Great God, Dil!" he rumbled. "Has everybody in the world gone nuts except me?"

"Maybe except me and thee, Sam. I haven't got much time. Look. Get hold of Captain Paris or Lieutenant Zeck. Tell them this. Tell them to get hold of the Washington people and tell them that Tram Widdmar is the kingpin of the organization. Tell them to grab him before he can run. Tell them that if they dig long enough and hard enough, they can find what they need."

"Tram Widdmar? What organization?"

"Just do that, Sam. They'll know what I mean."

"Dil, don't hang up. I can get you out of the country."

"Thanks, Sam. Not yet."

I hung up and stood in the gloom of the apartment. One thing was taken care of. One small thing, and maybe that wouldn't work. Maybe no one would believe me. I went back out to the car. I tapped a cigarette on the horn button and used the car lighter. The slow minutes went by. I was making a guess. A long-shot guess. The chain of reasoning was pretty tenuous. First, it had to be Tram, Mr. A, that Straw Hat would try to contact. Sammy would try to wake up Tram. Sammy would cut Tram loose. Tram would give Straw Hat the word. Blasting me on the street, in Tram's car, would be poor policy. They would want to get me into a safe place before doing it. They had Jill in a safe place. The easiest way to get me there would be to pretend to be willing to make a deal. And once I was there, it would be a lot more to the point to extract information from me before the inevitable erasure. That left me one course of action. To pretend to go along with Straw Hat, without suspicion, and take any chance I could find.

The more I thought about it, the less I liked it. They weren't going to take chances with me. And I had no training in this sort of thing. I was strong and quick, but there are tricks in every trade. I might do Jill more harm than good.

The courage born of anger ebbed fast, and uncertainty began to take over. The plan was stupid. I was casting myself as the indomitable hero, master of all situations. His strength was as the strength of ten . . . It was the sort of plan of action you can make after seeing too many Errol Flynn movies.

I opened the door and stepped out onto the street, with some half-baked idea of concealing myself and then trying to follow Straw Hat, even though I suspected that tailing him would be a trick even a professional couldn't manage.

Straw Hat came around the hood of the car. I took a step backward, sensed somebody behind me, half turned, and saw a heavy man in a dark, warm suit and a felt hat. He was silhouetted against that part of the sky which held the last pink glow of sunset, and I could not see his features.

"Sorry we took so long," Straw Hat said. "Get in the car."

They both moved closer. I looked across the street. I could barely see the brown-armed girl, still in the window. Her boy friend had gone. She was not looking toward us. A stoop-shouldered musician was trudging by, carrying a trumpet case, watching the sidewalk a yard in front of his toes.

"We can talk right here," I said.

"We can talk better in the car." All of Straw Hat's uncertainties were gone. The toy had been wound up again, the spring tight, the shiny wheels spinning.

"Don't make us put you in the car. That's childish, Bryant."

He opened the door. I got in. He pushed against my shoulder and I slid over into the passenger's seat. The man in the dark suit got into the back. Straw Hat got behind the wheel.

"We're going to make a deal," Straw Hat said.

"Maybe I won't like the terms."

"We release the girl. A man is going to commit suicide. He'll leave a note confessing to three murders. We'll give you ten thousand cash. In return, you tell us where the paper is. We'll hold you until we have it, then turn the two of you loose."

"If I could take your word, it would sound good."

I tensed as he casually yanked the gun from the shoulder holster. He tossed it in my lap. It slid down between my thighs.

"There's a guarantee of good faith, Bryant."

I picked it up. It was an automatic, not a large caliber. It fitted into my hand with vicious efficiency.

"Don't wave it around. Put it away."

I put it back in my lap. I found the clip catch. The clip was full. I pushed it back into place. I pulled the slide back, eased it forward. He reached over and clicked the safety on.

"Satisfied?"

"Yes," I said. I wasn't satisfied. I had the feeling that the weapon was just about as deadly as a Roy Rogers cap gun. It isn't much work to remove the firing pin from some automatics. "Where is the Townsend girl?"

"We'll take you there now."

"Where is she? As long as we're going there, is there any harm in telling me?"

"She's in a shack about halfway between Westwego and the Huey P. Long Bridge. Does that keep you happy?"

He started the car. For all his personal dainty precision, he was a poor driver. He had no driving rhythm.

I kept trying to push my right foot through the floor boards. He raced the motor and slipped the clutch whenever he shifted. And once again I found myself heading out Airline Highway. He turned down into Jefferson Highway and then went three quarters of the way around the circle and gunned the car for the bridge. The man in the back seat did not speak. I turned and looked at him. He sat in the middle of the seat, leaning forward, his hands on his knees. Street lights flicked across a flat expanse of cheek, a flat wedge of nose.

At the crossroads on the far side of the river we turned left toward Westwego. He tromped hard on the gas and kept the pedal down. It is desolate country, flat, wet, swampy, overgrown with scrub. The small houses were set in clearings that had been halfheartedly hacked out of the scrub. Our headlights struck the clots of mist that drifted across the narrow highway. There was still enough light in the western sky to pale the orange-yellow of the windows in the small houses.

I knew that I had to find out, before we arrived.

The motor roar was loud. I slipped the gun out of my lap and held it pointing down, wedged between the seat and the side of the door. The motor noise and wind roar muffled the sound of the safety as I clicked it off. I pulled on the trigger. I could barely hear the louder click. I slid the gun back into my lap.

"How much farther is it?" I asked.

"Half a mile."

Once the car stopped I was through. A nice unmarked grave back in the scrub. And a lot of unpleasantness before I could fill it. Very possibly a double grave. I wondered what would happen if I yanked on the wheel. We were going about sixty-five. Their chances of living through it were just as good as mine. Maybe one in 20.

I shifted my left leg closer to him, pulled it back a bit. There was a second thing that could be done. He would start to slow down when we were approaching the place. I doubted that Jill was there. To slow down, he would first take his foot from the gas. I watched his right foot in the reflected glow of the dash lights. I re-

versed the automatic so that I held it by the barrel.
This was going to give me a better chance, I hoped. Not
a good chance, but a better chance. I risked a quick
look in the back. The dark-suited one still sat as before.

Just as I looked back, Straw Hat took his foot off
the gas. I slammed my left foot on the brake as hard as
I could, jamming it down to the floor, and in the same
split second I moved forward so that my right shoulder
was braced against the dash, my head against the glass.

A Ford has enormous brake-band surface in relation
to its weight. The big man in the dark suit came forward over the seat like a projectile. Figure it out. We
were going sixty-five and I locked the wheels. Dark Suit
kept right on going sixty-five. That's about a hundred
feet a second. One eighth the speed of a .45 slug. I had
planned to hit him with the automatic as he lurched
forward. But the force pinned me so firmly against the
dash that I couldn't lift my arm. Besides, there was no
need of it. He tried to drive the rear-vision mirror out
through the windshield with the top of his head, before
falling face down between us. It all happened in fractional
parts of a second. Yet each fragment seemed clearly
divided from the other fragments of disaster. Across the
man's broad back, I could see Straw Hat fighting an
oddly misshapen steering wheel, his mouth sagging open.
My foot had slid off the brake and the unconscious man
pinned my left leg with his weight. The car was still moving, probably at about thirty miles an hour. I tried to hit
Straw Hat with the automatic. I missed his head and
hit his shoulder. As I tried again, and as he lifted his
right arm to protect his head, the left wheels of the car
dropped off the side of the road. It was enough of a
drop to wrench the wheel out of his left hand. The car
dipped down into the ditch and the soft dirt wrenched
the front wheels to the right. I felt the car going over
and tried to brace myself. It seemed to go over very
slowly. For one instant I floated toward Straw Hat, then
we struck and I was hammered down against him. Up
and down lost all meaning. Something smashed against
my head. I was probably out for not longer than two or

three seconds. I came to in a dark world. A silent world. The lights were out and the motor was dead. My left cheek was against a cool metallic surface and something heavy was across the backs of my thighs, doubling me up into an awkward position. Insects made a sing-song in the night, and the smell of vegetation was damp and heavy.

A droning sound came from a remote distance. It increased into a shrill roar, then whipped by with a flash of reflected light, a ripping sound, a diminishing moan into the distance. The reflected light gave me a chance to orient myself. The car was back on its wheels. The door on the driver's side was open. My cheek was on the running board. My legs were canted up on the seat, with the weight across them. I tested my arms. They worked. Three cars went by, close together. As they did so, I lifted my head. Straw Hat lay crumpled face down in the bushes, his heels a foot from my face. I judged we were about fifty feet from the highway, and the dim-ness of the light reaching me indicated that we must have rolled across brush that had sprung up again. I gingerly touched my head. Over the left ear was a long swollen welt, damp to the touch.

I grasped the chrome edge of the narrow running board with my hands and pulled myself forward. I wrig-gled my legs and made a few more inches. I reached out into the blackness and found the base of a bush, grasped the main stalk, and pulled myself farther. There was a thud and shift of weight behind me and my legs came free. I crawled out on my hands and knees, then stood up and leaned against the side of the car. A truck pounded by, and I saw the crushed and dented roof of the car. I found a match and leaned back in and lit it. The heavy man had slid part way to the floor. His hat was off. His bald head was inches from the brake pedal. I looked at the top of his bald head and all I could think of was that silly story about how Columbus made an egg stand on end. The match burned my fingers and I dropped it. I reached in and forced myself to touch his body. When gases trapped in his body made a distinct sound, I yanked my hands back. It was several seconds before I could continue. He had, as I had hoped, a gun. It was a stub-barreled revolver and it was crammed into his hip pocket. I ripped it free. The mosquitoes had begun to tell all their friends. Little darts of fire were piercing my neck and bare arms and ankles.

I rolled Straw Hat over and lit another match. Blood had run from the corner of his mouth. He was breathing. I found his pulse. It was strong and steady. I searched him. He had no other weapon.

Maybe it was hysteria. I felt the laughter well up in me. I couldn't stop it. It came out. It hurt my throat, strained my taped ribs. I fell helplessly back against the side of the car. The laughter made a flat, harsh sound in the night. I was laughing at everything in the world, and mostly at one Dillon Bryant, who happened to be dumb enough and clumsy enough to remove these two professionals from the field of operations.

I had stopped thinking clearly. I plunged through the thin line of brush and fell to my knees in the ditch, still laughing, holding the revolver in my hand. I climbed up onto the highway and headed in the direction we had been going, my left arm clamped around my middle to hold tight the pain of the crazy laughter.

The headlights coming behind me brought me back to my senses. I shoved the gun in my pants pocket. I tried to walk as though I were from one of the houses, as though I were taking an evening stroll. After it had gone by, I tucked the shirt inside Tram's voluminous trousers, opened the last visible button, and shoved the revolver in to lie against my skin. I wondered why I hadn't put a bullet in the back of Straw Hat's head. For someone accused of killing two, and who had actually killed one, what would another one matter? It wouldn't be like killing a person. It would be merely like breaking the spring on a wind-up toy.

Peepers chanted in the swamplands. The stars began to look bright. The heavy air was saturated with moisture.

Ahead, on the left, I saw the feeble light of the first house. I approached it cautiously, angled toward it, and picked my way across a yard littered with junk. I moved to the side of the house, edged over to the window, and looked in. A woman in a dirty slip lay on her back on a couch, reading a comic book. A naked kid played on the linoleum floor. A stringy man with yellowish skin slept in a rocking chair, stripped to the waist. They were tuned in to a quiz show. I could hear a voice saying, "Now, our contestants don't know this, folks, but that bag hanging there is filled with thirty pounds of whipped cream." And then he laughed like everything.

I backed away into the darkness and headed out toward the road. I'd gone only a few steps when, right behind me, I heard a sound like water being sucked down an open drain. I spun just as the monstrous dog came streaking toward me, low to the ground, moving with unmistakable intent. I started to run backward. Just as he jumped for my face, my heels hit something and I went over backward. I had only a moment's glance at him when he sped through the light that shone from the window, enough to see the unbelievably heavy mastiff head.

He went over me and landed in jangling trash. I scrambled to my feet and heard his low snarl as he came at me again. There is a way to handle a killer dog. As he springs for your throat, you must grab a front paw as he rises from the ground and then spin and hurl him with all your strength in the direction of the leap. But I wasn't going to be able to see a front paw, much less grab it.

The front door slapped back against the frame shack and an oblong of orange light shone out into the yard.

"Mack!" the stringy man snapped.

The dog skidded to a stop two feet from me, his shoulder muscles tensed, a rumbling snarl in his throat. I could see him clearly now. I backed away. The dog moved at the same speed.

"What you doin' in my yard?" the stringy man demanded.

I turned and gave him what I hoped was a reassuring smile. "Got the wrong house, apparently. No harm done, is there?"

The woman in the dirty slip stood behind the man,

132

bent a little so that she could peer under the arm he had braced against the doorframe.

"What house you want?"

"The next one up the line, I guess."

I had the feeling of loss. I pulled my left forearm against my stomach. The revolver was gone. I had apparently lost it when I fell.

"When the dog chased me, I fell. I lost something. You got a light so I can look for it?"

"Got a lantern," he said grumpily. "Git the lantern, May." He moved slowly out into the yard.

"Some dog you got there."

"Have to keep him chained daytimes. What you lose, mister?"

"Cigarette case. Had it in my hand."

The mosquitoes were after me again. They didn't seem to bother the lean, hollow-chested man. The woman came out with the lantern. The dog's eyes showed green in the light, green with a tinge of yellow. The lantern chimney was badly smoked, and she held it away from her side as she padded, barefooted, across the bare cindery dirt of the yard. The light escaped around the tin top of the lantern. A beam of it struck her hand that grasped the wire handle. It shone on the handmade silver ring I had brought from Venezuela and given to Jill Townsend. Jill had had it made smaller to fit the third finger of her right hand. The woman had it on her little finger. The light touched her vacant doughy face, her eyebrows puckered to a hairline, the shapeless body that stretched the sleazy slip.

Chapter Fifteen

THERE ARE moments when time, as a progression from one incident to the next, ceases to exist. I saw the ring on her hand, and it was as though we were three figures in a diorama, one of those little three-sided boxes. We were frozen there, and would remain there forever, for museum visitors to come and peer in at our little box and exclaim at how real the dog looked.

It was akin to what is supposed to happen in the mind of a man during the instant of death. During that frozen moment I relived the days from the moment of receiving Jill's letter up to the present moment. And the ring was somehow a symbol of everything that had happened. Jill's ring, forced onto a pasty finger—just the way my life and Jill's life had been forced into a new pattern, a pattern of strangeness and violence, with unreality superimposed on the sanity of everyday living much like a double-exposed negative.

I moved back to where I had fallen. The dog retreated, maintaining that same spacing between us. I saw that I had fallen over a rusted bedspring. I turned so that I kept the shadow of my body on the place where the revolver might be. I saw it, the curved butt protruding from a coil of the spring. The dog snarled as I bent over and grasped it. My idea was to spring back and shoot the dog, to pick the gun up slowly and then explode into action.

As I pulled the gun free, the dog sprang without a sound, ignoring the man's sharp command. He jumped not at my throat, but at my right wrist. His jaws closed on my wrist, not hard enough to break the skin, but hard enough to hold me absolutely motionless, as though caught by a vise.

The woman moved to the side and the lantern made oiled blue highlights on the gun. The man cursed softly and said, "Drop it, mister." It dropped back onto the springs. He bent over and picked it up and said conversationally, "Leggo, Mack."

The dog released my wrist and backed away, still intent on me. I wiped my wet wrist on the side of the linen trousers. My fingers were slightly numbed and they prickled as the circulation flowed back into them.

"What ya doin' in my yard with a gun?" the man demanded.

"I came for the girl. I wasn't sure which house it was."

"Hole up that light, May," the man demanded.

She took a step nearer me and held the light high. The man studied my face. "Where's the big car ya come in?"

"Down the road a way," I answered truthfully.

"Who sent ya?" he demanded.

"A sandy-haired man with a sunburned nose, about this tall. He couldn't come and he sent me. I wasn't sure of the house. That's why I came in and looked in the window. He'd described you and I was coming around to the door when that damn dog came at me."

"What's my name?"

"You know better than to use names."

"S'on the mailbox, anyways, Sipe," the woman said, speaking for the first time. Her voice was nasal. "Ain't I seen him somewheres?"

"How the hell do I know?" he said irritably. "I don't like none of this. There's no girl here, mister."

"Then where did your wife get her ring, Sipe?"

The woman made a small gasp and covered the ring with her left hand. Sipe turned sharply toward her. "Didn't I tell you not to take nothing off her?"

"Yes, but——"

He swung a lean arm at her. His hard palm cracked across her mouth and she fell down. The lantern went out. Sipe cursed her. "Git up and git on in the house, May," he said softly when his anger had run out.

"You better bring your car up here, mister."

"I can walk her down to it," I said.

He laughed without mirth. "She ain't doin' much walkin' tonight. You got the rest of the money?"

"How much was it supposed to be?"

"Goddamnit, don't you try knockin' down the price. You people know my price. I got a good place here. Lots of important folks haven't been leery about my price. And I never had no woman here before, and I don't like that. Women, they run off at the mouth. Say, I'm sorry about my woman takin' that ring. She's got an eye for pretties."

"How much more do we owe you?"

135

"Two hundred and fifty dollars," he said, with a warm
smack of his lips.

We went to the doorway. I stood with my back to
the road and counted out the money. Tram's money.
He took it, folded it, and stuffed it in his pants pocket.

"What'd the gal do?" he asked. "You don't have to
tell me, you don't want to. But I kinda wondered, her
being young like that. Why're they after her?"

I reached out and took the gun out of his hand, saying,
"Pardon me." The dog growled in the darkness.

"Shut up, Mack," he said.

"You don't have to know what she did," I said.

He shrugged. "Just wondered. Come on in, mister."

The naked child gave me a wide-eyed look. Sipe examined the lantern, hoisted the mantel, relit it, and adjusted the flame. "I can git her while you bring the car
up, mister."

"I'll come with you."

"Suit yourself. Let's go." I followed him back through
a sour kitchen and dirt-floored woodshed. He had the
soft tread of an animal. Behind the house was a narrow
yard, and a path leading directly into the brush. The
song of the peepers grew louder. The narrow path was
winding, and branches reached out from either side. I
heard the dog snuff loudly behind me. We came to an
open place and directly ahead was an expanse of black
stagnant water. He held the lantern high.

"Can't beat this place, mister. Had some real big
shots glad to rest up here. Safe as churches. Can get out
by boat or car or trail back through to Lake Catouatche.
Now, step careful. The catwalk's about six inches under-
water and narrow. Step right where I step."

I followed him across to the small island. Oily ripples
flowed away into the darkness with each step. The catwalk felt greasy underfoot, and it was about seventy
feet long. My shoes squelched loudly in the night silence as we came out on the muddy shore of the island.
It was barely big enough to hold the shack with dark
windows. Sipe shouldered the door open and put the
lantern on the table in the center of the room. There

136

were two double bunks, a kerosene range, and an ancient ice chest.

The small figure in the bottom of the farthest double bunk looked ominously still. She was dressed in the same outfit she had worn to the party where I had first met Laura. Mexican half blouse of white lace. Hand-painted skirt. Sandals.

I went over to her and shook her. "Jill!" I said sharply. Her head lolled loosely. In the lantern light her face was oily with perspiration, and her color was sick. Her dark hair was matted and tangled, the blouse filthy, the skirt stained, a jagged angry-looking tear in the soft cheek, not deep, but obviously inflamed.

"Pretty damn short stay for this one," Sipe said. "Fella said he gave her a shot so she'd get some rest and said it'd keep her out till tomorrow sometime. Look, now. I better carry her and you take the lantern. I'll go ahead. I could cross that walk with my eyes closed."

He reached into the bunk, slid one lean arm under her knees and the other under her shoulders, and lifted her out. Her head tilted back loosely and her free arm swung.

Sipe stood facing me, Jill in his arms. He gave me a wide grin that showed his mossy teeth, and held her a bit closer so that he could cup her breast with his big yellowed hand. "Like to kep' this bit around a while," he said, winking at me.

I turned away, my jaw shut so tightly that my teeth ached. I picked the lantern off the table and said, "Well, let's go."

I yanked the door shut behind me. When he got to the edge of the water he shifted her in his arms, put her face down over his right shoulder so that he could clamp her legs in his right arm and leave his left arm free for balance. I walked closely behind him. Jill's arms hung straight down. Her head swung against his back with each step he took.

Twenty feet along the narrow path he stopped so abruptly that I ran into him. The dog, who had waited for us to come back across the catwalk, growled softly at my heels.

"What's the matter?" I asked.

"Git off the path," he whispered. "Somebody coming." He crouched and moved sideways with his burden into the brush. He lowered the girl quickly to the ground, snatched the lantern, and blew it out. I saw the dancing beam of the flashlight coming.

"Who's that?" Sipe called.

The flashlight winked out at once. "Where's the girl?" a voice demanded thirty feet away. I recognized Straw Hat's voice.

"This here fella come to git her."

"Man with a shirt with fish on it?"

"Yeah. Fella you sent."

"He's the law, Sipe."

I heard the sudden harsh suck of Sipe's breath. By then I had the gun in my hand. I rammed the barrel against him and said, "One word to that dog of yours and I pull the trigger. Listen, Sipe. You've been suckered. You've been pulled into a bad rap. Why do you think this girl was brought here unconscious? This is a kidnaping pitch. This brings in the F.B.I. She's a reporter for the *New Orleans Star News*. Her name is Jill Townsend."

"Answer me, Sipe!" Straw Hat called.

"They told me she was wanted. They told me she was on the run," Sipe whispered, his breath coming short.

"I'm not the law. Play on my side, Sipe, and I'll see if I can get you out of this."

"I got the girl right here," Sipe called. "Come on down the path and we'll talk it over."

"Don't cross me, Sipe," Straw Hat called, and he was closer.

Sipe moved back into the path. I couldn't see him in the blackness. He muttered to the dog. I heard the hard running pad of feet, the familiar sound as of water swirling down a drain. The flashlight winked on and the beam caught the running dog, caught Sipe crouched in the center of the path. It was in slow motion. The black deadly leap of the dog. There was a shrill frightened cry from Straw Hat, and it was punctuated by the full-throated blam of a shotgun as the flashlight, still lighted, dropped to the ground and pointed off at right angles to the path.

My ears were ringing. I heard a rolling and thrashing, a deep snarling, a snap and chomp of jaws. Then there was a rising scream that stopped so abruptly the back of my neck turned to ice. There was no more thrashing in the path.

"Lantern," Sipe said in an odd, choked voice. I reached around in the darkness until I touched the hot glass. "Light it," Sipe said.

I burned my fingers fumbling for the thing that levered up the mantel. The first match sputtered out. I touched the wick with the second match and got the mantel back down. The flame grew. As the light spread I saw Sipe sitting in the middle of the path, his knees pulled up, his thin arms laced across his stomach.

The dog came slowly down the path, tongue lolling, eyes agleam.

Sipe turned toward me and his lips pulled back away from his teeth. "Hell of it—is—my own gun." He lowered his forehead slowly onto his knees. His shoulders hunched and tightened. Then he relaxed all at once and tipped over onto his side, toward me, uncoiling just enough so that I could see where the charge had got him, right in the pit of the stomach.

The dog stood and looked at Sipe. He lowered his head and nuzzled Sipe. He whined softly. He nuzzled him again, whining louder. Then he raised his muzzle toward the stars and gave a long, baying howl. As his head came down he fixed me with his eyes. The great shoulders tensed. I could almost feel him reasoning to a conclusion. While he had been occupied with the other stranger, this stranger had hurt his beloved master. It is odd to love a dog for his enormous loyalty, and yet hate and fear him at the same time. I couldn't risk the muzzle waver of a double-action shot, so I softly cocked the hammer. The click was loud in the stillness. I saw the dog gathering himself for the spring. I had no choice in the matter. After the hollow tone of the shotgun, the revolver sounded thin and sharp. The shot drove him back on his side. He turned and bit at his own flank.

The second shot stilled him. His legs made a feeble running motion and then he was still. The massive head rested on Sipe's thin shank.

I carried Jill up the path the way Sipe had carried her, the lantern in my left hand, her right hip warm against the side of my throat and my cheek. I did not want to look at Straw Hat. I tried to step over him without looking directly at him, but I couldn't. I went on with long strides, and I gagged, and barely kept from being ill.

May stood at the end of the path in doughy immobility.

She stared at me. Then she went running down the path in the darkness, crashing through the brush. When I reached the road I could hear thin distant screams mingling with the insect song, the wail of the tree toads, the thick grunt of a tug on the river. I walked up to where the car was. Cars slowed as they saw me, then speeded up. No Samaritans. Just nice clean careful people. Stay out of jams. Avoid anything that might lead to a courtroom.

I shifted her so that I held her across my two arms. A truck was coming. I stepped out into the lane when it was still two hundred yards away. I faced the oncoming lights, standing still with Jill in my arms.

The air brakes chuffed and heavy tires screamed. As he neared me he swung into the other lane, still braking. He stopped fifty feet beyond me. I walked up to the high door of the cab. It swung open and a wizened monkey face stared down at me.

"You crazy? What's the matter with her?"

"An accident."

"Swing her up here." I did so. He reached down and grabbed her slack arms and pulled her up into the seat. I climbed up, supporting her between us. A man in the narrow bunk behind the seat was snoring loudly.

I waited until he had worked his way up through the gears to cruising speed. I said, "I don't want cops in on this. It might be embarrassing to the lady."

"She's hurt, isn't she? You got to report accidents, guy!"

"Not hurt. Tight."

"How about her face there?"

"Just a scratch. Look, I'll give some money for your trouble. Are you heading across the bridge?"

"Uh-huh."

Jill had slumped over against my left shoulder. I got the wallet out. There was one more fifty, and a pack of smaller bills. I took the fifty out and held it down to where the dash lights showed the denomination.

"How about taking me far enough into town so that I can get a cab?"

"I ought to take you to the highway patrol."

"This is a fast fifty dollars. You won't be in any trouble over it."

"I got to make miles. This load is for Houston."

"I'll add a twenty and make it seventy. That's the top."

He looked at me. The wizened face cracked into a grin. "You know something? You just about convinced me."

The truck pulled away from us. Fortunately Jill was small enough so that I could support her against my side, her feet just clearing the sidewalk. I reached across my chest with my left hand and put my fingertips under her chin to keep her head from sagging onto her chest. In the darkness we could be mistaken for a slightly tipsy couple. Tipsy and amorous.

The problem was where to take her. I had three keys on the chain. The apartment Laura had found with Jill's help, the apartment where Talya had died, and Jill's apartment. My place would probably be watched. There might still be a police guard at the Harrigan apartment. And I felt very uneasy about going back to Jill's place.

Suddenly I remembered the disagreeable woman who had charged me Mardi Gras rates for the motor-court room out on Gentilly. I sweated as I walked Jill across the street to the cab stand. The driver swung the back door open.

"Upsy-daisy!" I said, swinging her in and onto the

141

seat. I got in, pushed her over on the leather-covered seat, and pulled the door shut.

The driver gave me a wise look. "Where to?"

"Now, you look like a man of the world," I said.

"Don't tell me. Let me guess. You lost your luggage and you and your wife want to find a nice room someplace." His voice was acid.

"A motor court or a nice little hotel, friend."

"And the lady is tired, eh?"

"Hell, she's passed out," I said.

"That makes it tough, and expensive."

"You're driving the car, friend."

He shrugged and put it in gear. The truck had brought us into the Broadmoor section. He drove over to Broad Street, headed up Broad to Bayou Road, and got onto Gentilly at the circle. I had half expected him to head that way. He didn't go as far out Gentilly as I had. He turned right into the arched entrance drive of a walled court.

"Give me twenty bucks and stay right there," he said. "I know this guy."

He left the motor running and went into the office. He leaned on the counter and talked to a broad, bald-headed man. Beyond the bald head I could see the wall clock. It was a shock to me that it should say only twenty to twelve, that it was still Monday, that it was still the same day I had spent so restlessly at Tram's house.

He came back out, whistling softly to himself, and drove into the court, looking for numbers on the small brown cottages. The place was planted with stubby palms. The fronds whispered against the side of the cab.

"Here it is. Number eighteen. Need any help with her?"

"Just go and unlock the door, friend."

I took a five out of my billfold before picking up Jill and edging out of the cab with her. He had turned on an overhead light, inside. I handed him the bill. He went whistling down the steps and drove off.

I caught the door with my heel and kicked it shut. I carried her to a dusty couch and put her down. It was a long narrow room with a draw curtain so that it could be changed into two rooms. The couch I had placed her on was of the kind that opens up to make a double bed. There was a double bed in the far end of the long room, and a bath that opened to the right near the bed.

It was an old place, stained with innumerable transients. It smelled of dust and damp rot. The walls were city-hall buff. I opened the door again, put the key on the inside of the lock, and locked the door. The place was hot and airless. But it was precious because it was refuge.

There was a bed lamp on the double bed. I carried her in and put her on the bed and turned on the bed lamp. I went back and turned out the overhead light, opened the two front windows, and pulled the draw curtain.

I went back and sat on the edge of the bed. The springs creaked loudly. I took her hand in mine. I didn't like her color, and I didn't like the way she breathed. Her pulse rate was an even fifty. Her hand felt as boneless as putty.

The sensible thing to do was get hold of that doctor she had called Jack. But she had never mentioned his last name.

Another choice was to let her sleep it off. That didn't sound good either. I decided that maybe I could get her back to life enough so that she could give me the doctor's name and number.

I unstrapped the sandals from her bare feet and set them on the floor. I took a look in the bathroom. There was a tub but no shower. I put the stopper in the tub and turned on the cold water. It ran out in a discouraged trickle, rusty against the stained porcelain. There were two discouraged towels, terry cloth with most of the little nubs worn off, gray rather than white.

The half blouse had three buttons at the side. When I had unbuttoned them, I pulled it off over her head. Her bra was so tight it cut into her back. I unhooked it and pulled it down over her limp, boneless arms. It left a depressed red line where it had encircled her. The Mexican skirt had one button at the left side and a concealed zipper. I went to the foot of the bed and got the hem and pulled it down off her slim legs. The panties were pale blue, like the bra, with an elastic around the waist and a thin border of gay yellow lace around the legs.

I put her clothes neatly on the chair. Her body was quite astonishingly lovely, with no roughness or coarseness of skin, no flesh sag. Her skin was like cream and her breasts were tipped with delicate coral pink. I looked upon her, and felt no desire, no guilt for looking at her as I did, only a sick fear that too much drug had been given her. To many minds the mere thought of a "nekkid woman" is erotic. There was nothing erotic about my thoughts as I looked down on her and tried to decide whether the shock of the cool water would help her or harm her. I compromised by going in and getting one of the towels and dipping it in cool water, wringing it out, and bringing it back to the bed. With it I rubbed away the dirt, the dried oil of perspiration. I turned her face down gently, half smiling as I saw the small raspberry mark, the mark shaped like a half-moon, like a tiny scimitar.

As the towel became soiled, I kept refolding it to disclose clean surfaces. I used hot water on the gash in her cheek. Once the crust of dried blood was gone, it looked a good deal less important.

I picked her up in my arms and carried her into the bathroom, clumsily rapping her bare ankle against the doorframe. I knelt with her beside the tub, lowered her into the cool water and raised her out quickly, lowered her again so that the water covered her, then raised her out. Too late, I remembered my wrist watch. The damage was done, anyhow. I watched her face and kept repeating the process until my arms felt as though they were going to drop off. I let her rest in the water for a time, and then started again. When her fingernails and lips began to have a faintly blue tinge, I carried her back to the bed, got the dry towel, and rubbed her down so briskly that her skin began to glow pink. Just when I was about to give up, her slack lips stirred. She made a complaining groan and tried to turn her face away from the light. I slapped the undamaged side of her face sharply. My fingers left red marks. She groaned again. She sounded like a cross child being awakened to catch the school bus.

No matter how I tried, I couldn't bring her out of it any further. I left her there, walked a quarter mile to a bean wagon, and came back with a quart of hot black coffee in a container. I held her head up and got some of the coffee down her throat. She choked weakly. I set the coffee aside, pulled her onto her feet, and supported her there. When I tried to walk her, her feet merely dragged. After several more slappings, several more sips of coffee, I tried again. Her feet worked weakly. She was taking steps. She made groaning complaints constantly, her chin on her chest, head lolling. But I was persistent and I was merciless.

Chapter Sixteen

MY WATCH would no longer run, and she had none, so I had no idea of how much time had passed before she began to walk supporting most of her weight, her chin a bit off her chest, her eyes still closed. And instead of groans she kept saying, "No. Lemme 'lone. Wanna sleep. No."

The last of the coffee I gave her was stone cold. I sat her on the edge of the bed and held her shoulders to keep her upright. She sighed heavily and her chin sank slowly back onto her chest.

I put my lips close to her ear. "Can you hear me, Jill?"

"Go 'way."

"Jill, listen to me! This is Dil!"

" 'Way," she muttered.

"Jill, honey! Where's your clothes? I can't find your clothes!"

She didn't stir. I was certain she had gone back to sleep. I held her shoulders and looked at her. Her right hand moved and went fumbling along her thigh. It slid up across her flat stomach to the warm well of her breasts.

She took a deep shuddering breath. Her head came up slowly and her eyes opened. A frown slowly grew on her forehead, pinching the jet-black brows together. Her eyes held a baffled, puzzled look.

"Dil!" she said thickly, drawling the one-syllable name.

"That's right," I said loudly, cheerfully, grinning into her face. "Don't you think you ought to help me find your clothes? Where did you lose them?"

Her arms went into the instinctive and classic posture of modesty, left arm across her breasts, her right hand making like a fig leaf. Dismay slowly appeared in the dazed eyes. I could have screamed murder at her until I was blue in the face, and she would not have stirred from her semiconscious state. By alarming a very basic part of her nature, I had done more than the cold water, coffee, slaps, and interminable walking could ever have done.

"What . . . you doing . . . here?" she demanded slowly and painfully. "Get out . . . of here!"

I released her shoulders and backed away. She swayed, but remained sitting upright. Her mouth grew firm. "Get out!"

"Not me, honey."

I respected her for the enormous effort it took her to get to her feet. She sidled carefully, glanced over her shoulder, and began to back to the bathroom door. The effort she was making and the shock to her emotions was bringing her out of it. I moved quickly and blocked her way, still grinning. She gave a cry of dismay, tottered to the bed, yanked the spread up, and crawled under it. She pulled it up to her chin and stared at me with wide, angry, blazing eyes.

"Damn you!" she said. Her voice was still thick. Tears gathered in her eyes.

I sat on the edge of the bed. She squirmed away from me. I said, "Look! You've *got* to wake up. This was the

146

only way I could bring you out of it. You were drugged."

Her eyes grew dull again. "Drugged?" she said.

"Yes. Can't you remember your apartment? Can't you remember being tied to the chair?"

"Tied to the chair?"

"For God's sake, stop repeating every word I say! Wake up!"

"Need . . . hot coffee, Dil."

"I'll get you some if you promise not to go to sleep."

"Promise."

I was gone about ten minutes getting the second quart. When I came in the bed lamp was off. I cursed her with feeling.

"I'm awake, Dil," she said in a small voice. "I was afraid you'd come back while I was still getting dressed."

She turned the light on. She was sitting up in bed. The dirty blouse was back on. I glanced at the chair. Just the skirt remained. She took the container and sipped, holding it in both hands. Then she gave it to me. I took a quick swallow and set it aside.

"Do you think you need a doctor?" I asked.

"No. I'm getting clearer all the time. Someone called on the phone. They pretended to be you. It frightened me. As I started to leave, those men came in. One of them was the one I saw that day when I left Laura. He twisted my arm. It still hurts. They tied me to that chair and he hurt my arm again. He wanted to know about the paper they want." She lifted her chin. "I didn't tell them a thing."

"You didn't know anything, did you?"

"I had a funny hunch Monday morning, Dil. It came from some little things rattling around in my mind. Little things that didn't fit. Like Laura saying that about things not being what they seem. And that rabbit she gave you and the way she bought it being so sort of coy, and not like her. So I went to that jewelry store, the big one there on the corner, and I talked to the manager and I described the rabbit. He said they'd never had anything in stock like that ever. Just in case you had the wrong store, I went to the others in the neighborhood. They'd never had any rabbits like that either. Dil, have you got it?

I'm almost certain that's what they want."

"Sure I've got it. But she came out of the store with it all gift-wrapped."

"That was window dressing, Dil. She bought something else and switched them before she gave you the package."

I took the rabbit out of my pocket. My key chain was through the loop on the top of his straight ear. I looked at every part of him. He looked solid. Jill reached over and took him. She paid close attention to the base, turning it this way and that in the light.

Her voice was excited. "Look at the base carefully, Dil. There's a little round depression there. You can't see it unless the light strikes it properly. Like a hole about a quarter inch in diameter had been drilled and then filled up again."

"But that's crazy! If she was planning to trade her information for security, why let me trot around Mexico with it?"

"One, she probably had it memorized anyway. Two, would you have been likely to lose a gift from your bride, along with the key to her apartment?"

"Whoever wanted it while I was in Mexico would have had to kill me to get it."

"Exactly. Laura was a lot of things, but not a fool. Not ever a fool, Dil."

"Then all the time their hunch was right, that hunch that I had what they wanted. Why wasn't Haussmann after it too?"

"I don't know where he fits. I only happened to get his name."

"He and Laura were both trying to trade this information for security."

"Probably he had it memorized too."

Her fingers closed around the rabbit. "What can it be, Dil? What can it be that's so important?" Suddenly she stiffened. "Wait! I'm still groggy. I'm taking too much for granted. Where are we? What is this dreadful room? How did you get me away from them?"

I had to start with Tram. As I expanded on what I

had seen him do, and the conclusions I had reached, her eyes narrowed and she began to nod.

"What are you nodding for?"

"Another hunch, Dil. You see, Barney told me something that I didn't tell you. He told me not to tell you. I asked him why, but he just smiled in that dusty way of his. He told me that if by any remote chance—and he spoke sarcastically—I happened to be letting you hide at my apartment, it would be nice if I urged you to go stay with Tram. I asked him if that was so he could catch you easier and he told me that I should just trust him and believe him. Do you see what my hunch is?"

"That they *wanted* me to go to Tram, all of them. That means Tram may have been under suspicion. What could they prove by my being there?"

"I don't know. Maybe the house was wired for sound, or something. What happened after you saw Tram talking on the dead line?"

I went on from there. I put in my own guess about Sipe, that he had operated a hideout for wanted people for a long time, and that Talya's friends probably put Jill there as a first step in taking over the entire operation. I told of the end of Sipe and of Straw Hat. I told of the car and how it turned over, and shooting the dog, and then about the truck driver and the taxi driver.

I said, "And that's how we got here."

"More detail, please. What did you do after you brought me here?"

"You gave me a bad time. I got your clothes off and gave you a cold sponge bath and then took you in and swashed you up and down in the tub about a hundred times, then poured coffee down you and walked you a couple of hundred miles. We got here before midnight. When I got that last batch of coffee, it was a little after three."

I thought I had seen the very best of her blushes. But this one was the color of mashed tomatoes. Her eyes were wide. "Jumping Judas," she said softly and with great awe.

I caught her hands. I said, "Look. When you dropped me at Tram's Sunday night, you were sore, weren't you?"

149

"Yes."

"I was the dumbest guy in the world. I didn't have the faintest idea why you were sore."

She looked away from me. "Didn't you?"

"No. Do you know what I had to do? I had to wade across a pond by lantern light and see you unconscious in that bunk before it began to make sense to me. I saw you there, and I remembered that cat you told me about. What was his name?"

"Oliver."

"And then I remembered a lot of funny things that should have been more evident to me. What a hell of a life for a one-man woman, watching the man go marry a thing like Laura!"

The blush remained in undiminished intensity, and she wouldn't look at me. "Did I say you were the man?"

"You don't have to say it. After that feeble kiss in your hallway, the only time I ever tried to kiss your lips, I had to say that the next guy would do better. That's what hurt you, isn't it?"

"How did you find out?" she whispered.

"Just by looking at you in that grubby hole of a hideaway and realizing what would be left of me if you were dead. Not a hell of a lot. A funny thing to find out at this point. A kid sister, you were. So now you creep up on me."

"Pity, Dil?" she asked, not looking at me.

"You're a very special person, Miss Townsend. Too special, I think, to get messed up with old Try-again Bryant."

She was looking over into the corner of the room, at something that wasn't there. The light touched the clean and pure line of her cheek. Her dark hair, where I had got it wet, had started to curl tightly.

"Don't run yourself down, Dil."

"Oliver, the cat, had sense. He picked you. You've got no sense."

"But I'm just as stuck as Oliver was."

"Then it's the only thing I can do, isn't it? Under the circumstances. How do you like tired old words? Song words? Movie words?"

She swung her eyes slowly around to meet mine. The blush had faded to pallor. Cool fingertips touched my cheek. "Old words are good words."

"I love you."

"Thanks for not qualifying it. Thank you, Dil, for just saying it. It probably sounds stiff and funny to you, hearing your own lips say it to me. But not to me. I've said it too often, said it too often to you. So it's familiar, and very dear. I love you, Dil."

She held her arms up like a child. The kiss began awkwardly. Noses in the way again. Her lips tightly compressed. According to the books it should have changed. But it didn't. I tried to make it change. She tried to conceal the involuntary flinch from the touch of my hands. She was tensed. It just wasn't any good. I let go of her. She sank back onto the pillow and looked up at the ceiling.

"No good," she said. "No good at all."

"Don't let it worry you. Things will improve."

"You . . . suppress something too long. What happens to you, Dil? What is it that happens? Inside me is a spring wound tight. It should come loose, but it's caught."

"There'll be plenty of time."

"And if the spring never came loose, would you stay around?"

"Of course."

"And end up hating me. Female icicle. Woman who endures patiently, and hates every minute of it. The world is full of women like that."

"They're like that because they want to be like that."

"Please, Dil. Try again."

I tried. I tried to carry it further, tried to carry it up to and beyond the point where she'd break. But I just succeeded in feeling like a heel. She tried too. But she couldn't even come up with an imitation of pleasure. I stood up. She lay looking at the ceiling, tear tracks on her cheeks, her face expressionless. I lit two cigarettes from the fresh pack I'd got with the coffee. I handed her one. She took a deep quivering drag on it and closed her eyes.

151

She said, "Let's just forget our little conversation."

"Not yet."

"My adoring Oliver is pretty indicative. Don't old maids love cats?"

"Don't forget I've been reviewing the merchandise. That would be too much of a waste to contemplate. Just let me chip away at that rusty spring."

"It won't work."

"This was a silly time to try, anyway. How do you know what that drug may have done to you? And there's another thing. My marrying Laura. That could make with quite a psychological quirk, you know."

"I can't even kiss you," she said in the forlorn tone of a lost child.

I bent over and rumpled her damp hair. "Forget it. Let's sleep. I'll take the couch over there. We can't do anything tonight, about our little present for the Jones boys. If you're right about people wanting to steer me to Tram's place, then all this man-wanted stuff is window dressing." I kissed her lightly on the cheek. "Have a good sleep."

I pulled the draw curtain across, found sheets in a bureau drawer, and made up the couch. I heard a lot of sloshing around in the bathroom and wondered what she was doing. As I was wondering, the sleep of utter exhaustion reached up with a black velvet hook and yanked me under.

A great roaring woke me up. It scared me so that I bounded out of bed, right in the middle of a seminightmare about being trapped in a tunnel with a train roaring down on me. It took long befuddled seconds to realize that it was raining so hard that the palm fronds were sounding like the steady crash of surf. I sat on the edge of the bed and had a cigarette while my pulse gradually slowed down. I went to the window. Beyond the steady curtain of rain was a faint grayness. The rain bounded on the window sill, and spattered cold on my thighs. There was no way of telling what time it was. Already the road in front of the place was a small lake. Deluge. Time to build the ark. Maybe too late to build the ark.

Just when it seemed that no rain could fall harder, the tone deepened and it came down so fast that the meager gray faded perceptibly. The air was cooler. I wondered if Jill, in her exhausted sleep, had kicked off the sheet and might be getting chilled. I padded around the edge of the curtain. I shut my eyes hard and opened them again. It didn't work. The bed was still empty. The bathroom door was open onto darkness.

I went to the bed and clicked on the bed lamp. It was watery yellow against the cheerless gray of the windows behind the bed. The note was on the pillow, the pencil stub beside it. The pencil had been on the tray on the bureau, I remembered. She'd used paper from one of the drawers for the note.

Darling,

I've decided that the safest way is for me to take friend bunny to the proper people. Please stay right here and maybe before you even wake up the authorities will be here presenting you with medals. I've borrowed money from you, which you may even get back. I'll make myself presentable and go see Barney first. I'll be terribly busy, darling, turning out scads of copy on all this, and I think that as soon as the formalities are over for you, you should let Sam send you back down with Paul. When you're in town again, don't forget to phone. People say odd things when they're utterly exhausted. I hope neither of us took it very seriously. Thanks for everything, Dil.

Love,
LITTLE SISTER

Chapter Seventeen

I DON'T KNOW how long I stood there with the over-sized note in my hand, with the rain roar filling the room.

I had no way of knowing when she'd left. I didn't like it. She had entirely too much confidence in herself, too much sense of safety and security in this city of hers, too much reliance on the meager invulnerability of her position. The events of the previous evening should have given her a more lasting case of nerves.

But somehow she had pulled herself together, set her jaw, and gone striding out to shoulder what she considered to be her share of the job. A perky, gutty little damosel and, I was afraid, not a very wise damosel. I knew at once that her failure to respond to me had something to do with her action. In a funny way, she was probably proving something.

The bad part of the note—the part that gave me the chills—was that bit about making herself presentable. That meant clothes. And that meant her apartment. She had had no purse when I found her. Then I remembered the key that was still on the chain affixed to the rabbit. I trotted back in and went through my pockets. The chain was still there. Her key and the rabbit were gone. The clothes I had borrowed from Tram were ruined anyway. Some rain wasn't going to make any difference. I dressed quickly. The revolver was going to get wet tucked in the front of the shirt. I swung the cylinder out. Three loads left. I put the hammer down on an empty chamber. I looked in the wallet. I had seven dollars left.

My shoes, soaked from Sipe's swamp, had dried enough to pinch. I tried to go out the door. Jill had locked it behind her. I yanked the window up, kicked out the screen, and stepped over the sill into water that came up over my shoes. I hunched my shoulders and splashed toward the arched entrance. Within seconds I was as wet as if I had rolled instead of walked. There was no one in the office. The night light was still on and there was a sign on the door telling which button to push to get service. The water loosened up the shoes so they didn't hurt any more. The clock in the office said ten after seven. The big road was a young river. Early traffic was creeping along, making waves like so many speedboats. Some cars and a city bus were stalled on the other side of the road. Headlights gleamed pallidly into the rain curtain. This rain was going to finish the world. In a few hours there'd be nothing but some heads bobbing around. I could feel the steady pressure of the rain on my shoulders. It was the kind of rain we had had in North Burma during the monsoon season. It hit you as if it had been dropped out of a bucket from a third-story window.

My chance of grabbing a cab was just as good as my chance of spreading my arms and flying. At the next bus stop a crowd was huddled under shelter, gleaming with pliofilm, staring at the world as though they wanted to trade it in on a new one.

I walked beyond the bus stop and up to the next light. I watched the cars at the red light until I found my man. He was hunched over the wheel, staring at the miserable world through thick lenses. His chin was a halfhearted suggestion. I opened the sedan door and slid in as he gave me a wide startled look. I chunked the door shut and beamed at him. "Nice of you to give me a lift on a morning like this."

"You're getting the seat all wet!" he said.

"I guess the damage is all done. Say, you got a green light."

He licked his underlip, put the sedan into gear, and moved slowly on, muttering softly to himself. He was probably a very nice guy. Candy for the wife and presents for the kiddies. A pat on the shoulder from the boss. "Nice reports this month, George." Maybe he had little daydreams where he repulsed rough strangers, cowed holdup men, and rescued blonde maidens. But

he couldn't quite bring himself up to the point of order-
ing me out of his car. Later he would tell himself that
it was a public-spirited thing to pick up a sodden stranger
on such a morning.

He drove cautiously down Canal. I said, "Say, you
can help me a lot if you make a left into the Quarter."

"I turn right on South Claiborne," he said haughtily.

"It's just a few blocks over. Everybody'll be late to
the office this morning. Bet some of them won't get
there at all."

He kept on mumbling, but he did edge over toward
the center island. He trundled the car across the tracks,
paused for traffic, and went down a narrow street of the
Quarter. Day had turned to dusk. The rain churned the
deep water in the streets and bounced high off everything that was out of water. New Orleans, through strenu-
ous effort, has managed to keep its feet dry most of
the time. But the subsurface water is always there. There's
no good place for a heavy rain to go. It has to be
pumped out of the drainage system over the levees and
into the river. When it rains too fast for the pumps,
you have a situation.

"How far?" George asked crossly.

"Oh, six more blocks."

"You're making me very late," he said.

"You'll never know how much I appreciate this."

He let me out a block from Jill's place. He could
have got closer, but with the one-way streets, this was
quicker. I got out and thanked him and walked ahead.
George gunned it and smacked me with a solid sheet of
water. I couldn't get sore at him. He had to get one
inning.

A blonde girl, student type, was walking in the rain
in a thin dress. She walked slowly, as if in a trance. Her
hair was plastered flat and the dress was like a heavy
coat of paint. Rain was doing something to her. She
looked at me with a sort of remote ecstasy, and mouthed
something that I couldn't understand because of the rain
sounds. Maybe she thought I was a kindred spirit. I was
moving slowly too, because I didn't want to go barging
up to Jill's door without knowing who was around and

about. I prayed that Jill had had the good sense to phone Barney Zeck before returning to the apartment.

I walked on. I glanced back over my shoulder. Student Type was standing, looking after me, her hands on her hips, feet planted wide. Not today, honey. Not any day, honey. Go get some sleep.

Nobody seemed to have any special interest in Jill's door. I gave a long ring and turned my back to the door and waited. Student Type came and struck her pose in front of me.

"God! The rain," she said.

"Go away, will you?"

"You love it, too. I know you do."

"Beat it, Sis."

"This is a day for madness. For rain goddesses. For a dark splendor."

"You better go dry off. You've got a fever." I turned and punched the bell button again.

She moved closer to me. She said, "They're watching you from across the way, Bryant. That's why I'm standing in front of you, you damn fool."

I took a better look at her. There was a quick, sharp intelligence in her eyes.

"Who's across the way?"

"Today we're making a clean sweep, Bryant. I'm short-handed because the Townsend girl came here, and my partner had to cover her. Some of the cars have stalled out. It's a mess. And that business last night was bad. You're making us move too fast."

"What do we do now?"

"Keep moving a bit, but not enough to get out in the clear. I don't know what they have in mind, but they might risk a shot if you stand still enough. I think they want to grab you, not shoot you. As long as I'm here, I'm fouling the works."

"How about walking up the street arm in arm?"

"I've watched the corner. There's a car I don't like parked up there, and another one I'm more certain of right down there. Don't stare. Sixty yards or so down the block."

"Who is rounding up whom?" I asked politely.

"Oh, the city is a bottle with a cork in it."

"That's nice to know."

"We've talked a long time. They'll be wondering. They picked up the Townsend girl."

"How nice!" I said. "That little document everybody's been so hot about is in her possession."

The sharp eyes grew wide and her lips parted. "Oh, no!" she said.

"Oh, yes!"

"Where would she get it? You didn't have it. We checked that."

"I had it and didn't know it."

She glanced up the street and tensed a bit. "We're going to have company, Bryant."

I looked up the street. Two men were walking down the street. They were moving too slowly for men walking in that kind of rain. I took the revolver out of my shirt. She glanced at it and grabbed it.

"You might have mentioned it," she said. She moved to the side, put the muzzle an inch from the lock, and blasted it. It packed the brass lock with lead. I worked the catch and took a dive at the door with my shoulder. It swung open and we went in fast. The last glance at the two men showed me that they had broken into a run.

I slammed the door. The lock was no good. There was a sliding bolt set into the frame. My thumb slipped off it the first time. I clicked it over just as a weight struck the door on the other side.

Student Type was already at the phone. She sat on the floor beside the phone table, the phone at her ear, waiting. She glanced at me and through me.

"Statch? This is Baker. You left me in a hell of a spot. Bryant showed. No. I haven't had a chance to ask him yet. We're in a state of siege in the Townsend apartment. But look. The hottest thing. You know, we let them take the girl, as per instructions. Did they take her where we hoped? Good! Statch, she has it. Yes. Just when we thought it didn't exist, she has to have it on her. Sure. I understand. 'By.'"

She hung up and winked at me, held out her hand. I pulled her to her feet. "We were hoping Widdmar would have to come out in the open on this one. He still thinks he's going to be able to make a run for it. His guard is down a little, so Jill Townsend was taken out there. This damn rain! I hate rain! No roundup has ever been so completely fouled up as this one, but on the other hand I guess they never had quite as much at stake before." She sighed and ran her fingers through her soaking blonde hair.

"Why did you let Jill be taken like that?" I demanded angrily.

"Look. It's hard to get something definite on a man like Widdmar. We had a job getting his house wired. We had to find Sammy a girl friend who would lure him out of the way while we planted the microphones. Then we gently guided you out there. It didn't work. It didn't give us a thing. You talked on that patio affair, out of range. We had a tap on his phone, and didn't catch the number that was dialed. The sounds of violence sent us scrambling in all directions. But you moved too fast, and got away from us. There's a lot I don't know. I'm just a little cog. I do know that they moved in on Sipe's place just about ten minutes after you left, and we've been hunting for you and the girl ever since. We were worried until we found they were watching this place. That meant Jill Townsend got away, and you probably got her away."

"What put you onto Widdmar?"

"Ancient history. A dossier. A big file. Then a couple of years of legwork. The whole local organization was pretty well documented when the Renner woman came in here and gave them a reason for going into action. Since then things have been confusing as hell, and you haven't made them any simpler. You should have been snared and put in a box as soon as you got back here from Mexico."

"Who killed the Morin girl?"

She ran her fingers through her hair again. "I got scared out there on the sidewalk. When I get scared, I talk too much. I've been talking too much. No more answers from me, Bryant. My people ought to be here by now."

We went to the front door, avoiding the view hole, and

listened. There was a brisk knock. "Who is it?" she demanded.

"Harley. Open up, Baker." She nodded to me. I snapped the bolt over and pulled the door open. It was the elder, bulkier of the two Jones boys.

"Hello again," I said.

He ignored me. The two men who had come running down the sidewalk were climbing into the back of a sedan. Two cars had converged on the car parked up the street. Two men and a woman were coming out of a doorway across the street, their fingers laced at the backs of their necks.

"So soon?" Baker said.

"The time has been moved up," Harley said. "Come on." We followed him up to a black sedan. A stranger sat behind the wheel. Baker and I got in the back, soaking the upholstery. Harley took his hand mike off the hook and reported in, stating that I had been taken into custody, adding that seven strangers had been pulled in. I didn't like being grouped with the strangers. Harley's words had a cool sound.

"Where are we going?" I asked.

"We're dropping you at the Federal Office Building, Bryant." He turned in the seat as the car moved slowly to the corner.

I made my voice as patient as I could. "Look. I have had what might be called a bad time. I have had my ribs busted. I have had shotguns go off in my face. I have had a knife held on me. I have found out that a guy I considered my best friend is no good. My wife was killed, and another girl was killed, and Haussmann was killed, and Siddman died, and Sipe was shot, and Straw Hat had his throat chewed out. I've killed a dog, for which I am sorry, and a man in a dark suit, for which I am not very sorry. All in all, I am beginning to lose my patience, Harley. You're heading for Widdmar's house. I would dearly like to go along with you. Maybe I've made you a lot of trouble, but where did you get the tip that Jill has that paper or document you want? How about it? If you say no, I'm going to open this door and get out, no matter how fast you happen to be going at the moment."

Harley looked at Baker. "Of all the china-shop bulls I ever saw . . ."

"We'll get there after the windup, anyway," Baker said convincingly.

"Five thousand guys in this town the Renner woman could have married," he said.

"Who found Haussmann?" I asked him.

"That one you call Straw Hat—we knew him as Smith—he could have answered a lot of questions."

"I didn't get him. The dog did. Besides, my next wife is going to be a newspaperwoman. Don't you want attractive coverage in the press for your noble efforts?"

"This may surprise you, Bryant. There's going to be no coverage at all. Just enough to clear you of three murders, and put Smith in your shoes, and have him killed avoiding capture. For the rest of it, nobody knows a thing."

"Let him come along, Harley," Baker said. "And give me your coat or something. I can't stop shivering."

Harley muttered something to the driver. We began to make better time. We hit the water hard enough to send solid sheets over onto infuriated pedestrians. The siren began to growl, to work its way up through the octaves. I glanced behind us and noticed that we were the lead car of a caravan.

By the time we straightened out on Airline Highway, the siren was a high-pitched, constant scream.

I yelled in Baker's ear, "How many are you rounding up?"

She gave me a wide-eyed shrug.

I could see that from now on I was going to be told less than nothing. I kept telling myself to relax. I kept telling myself that they wouldn't take any silly chances with Jill's life. I tried to lean back in the seat, but I kept hunching forward as though I could make the car go faster.

As we slewed hard and hit Tram's drive, the siren off, Baker said, "I told you so. All over but the stenographic reports."

I had underestimated the number of people involved. There were five cars already in Tram's drive. We made three more. Harley and Baker got out. The driver stayed where he was. They seemed to have forgotten me. I followed them in. The front door was wide open.

As we went down the hallway, I heard Tram's booming voice. "Now, look! All this is completely ridiculous! Those two men brought Miss Townsend here. I didn't send for her. They forced their way in here, waving a gun in my face."

They were gathered in the big lounge. Tram looked brown and rubbery and innocently worried. Two men stood against the wall, their hands at the backs of their necks. Jill sat in a deep chair, her face green pale. Tram was pacing and waving his arms.

A man with crisp white hair, a lean, distinguished face, and an air of authority said mildly, "Come now, Widdmar. This merely delays things. I assure you that we have enough."

One of the men standing by the wall said in a heavy accent, "He is right. We forced our way in here. He protested."

Jill met my glance and smiled weakly. She looked at the man who could have been cast as a society lawyer by Metro. "Mr. Widdmar knew I was being brought here," she said firmly.

"Is that any way to treat an old friend, Jill?" Tram complained.

She turned her smile on him. "I'm the old friend who first smelled something odd about you, Tram, and turned your name in nearly three years ago. Something odd about you and about your habits and—when you're off guard—your way of thinking."

Tram still looked like a cupid with a faint leer, but his eyes changed. His eyes changed to the eyes of a man who could do murder. And I remembered something. A funny thing. When it happened, it had gone right over the surface of my mind. But it had left a faint trace.

I went up behind the gray-haired man, pulling away from Baker's restraining hand. I said, "If you want to clip him with something, would murder be all right?"

162

The man turned sharply. His eyes widened. Then he grew angry. "Who brought this man here?" he demanded. He glared at Harley.

"Hi, Dil," Tram said softly, smiling.

"Please let me talk to you alone," I said to the man.

He shrugged. I followed him into Tram's bedroom. "What's on your mind, Bryant?"

"What will happen to Widdmar? I mean with what you have on him?"

"He's a citizen. A treason trial is a pretty delicate thing. He has money. It's very hard to say, Bryant."

"Look. When I was here, before I suspected Tram, we talked about Laura. I talked too much. I think he put something in my drink. Anyway, he said that maybe pliers and a wire coat hanger wasn't a very merciful way to die. Zeck knew pliers had been used. Zeck told me. It wasn't in the paper. So how would Tram know?"

He shook his head slowly. "That isn't enough. It's a pleasant idea to pin that on him, but it isn't enough to go on. Besides, maybe the one who did it told him exactly how it was done. Smith was the assassin. We know he killed the Morin girl."

"Do those boys change their methods? Why didn't he use the same method on Laura?"

"That's a pretty feeble point, Bryant. I can't waste any more time on this."

There was a brisk knock at the door. The society lawyer opened it and he was handed something. He examined it closely, his back to me. Then he turned toward me. He was hard-eyed and exultant. His hands were shaking. I saw that he held the rabbit, a tiny metal capsule, and a long thin strip of onionskin paper inscribed with tiny printing.

"The first real break," he said softly. "The first genuine break in far too many years. See this? A nice list. Names and cities. About fifty of our cities, and the name of the kingpin in each one. The co-ordinator. The nice respectable citizen trying to put his knife in our back."

"Is Tram's name there?"

He squinted at the list. "Yes."

"Will that help you jail him?"

He gave me a sad smile. "Who is going to testify to the authenticity of this list? It doesn't give us a list of people to jail. It gives us a list of people to watch. A lot of them will have gone underground by now. A lot of these names are familiar. And a lot of them will prove to be people considered above suspicion. You can see why it was worth making an effort, Bryant. This little piece of paper explodes a system that took probably fifteen years to twenty-five years to build."

"Then why not run a bluff on Tram Widdmar? He's probably pretty rattled by now. Does he know Smith is dead?"

The society lawyer stared at the far wall and pursed his lips. He shrugged. "Nothing to lose, I guess. But he's too clever. It won't work."

We went back in. Busy little men were going through every page of every one of Tram's books. He was watching them with ill-concealed contempt.

The white-haired man said, "Widdmar, what Bryant has told us, added to what we already know, gives us a very interesting line of investigation. I think we'd better turn you over to the local police."

"For what?"

"For the murder of Tilda Renner. You spoke too freely to Bryant about a pair of pliers being used. And Smith is eager to make a trade. We have the evidence on him for the murder of the Dvalianova girl. He seems to think he can give us enough so that you can be convicted of the murder of the Renner woman. Personally, I think that would be a very nice solution. Neat, so to speak."

Tram laughed aloud. "Don't try to bluff me."

He seemed as much at ease as though he were surrounded by his friends at one of his own parties. He dropped into a big chair and beamed at all of us.

Jill stood up. She turned toward Tram. "And I'll testify too, Tram. You see, I saw you come out of the apartment that night. I didn't know then that you'd killed her."

The room was very still. Tram's face changed. His brown hand slid up from between the cushion of the chair and the side of the arm. He reached Jill in one quick bound before anyone could move. He spun her around.

He said, "I'm walking out of here. Don't try anything at all, or I'll blow a hole in this girl's spine."

He pushed her forward and we drew back, all of us. He moved slowly and carefully.

"You won't get far," the white-haired man said gently.

"I might. The Renner woman contacted me here. She said she had the list and she was going to trade it with you people. I sent word back and then got orders. She let me in that night when I said I had a good offer for her. I killed her and let Smith in to search the place. And all the time you had it, Bryant. Move away from the door, Bryant, my old dear friend. My stupid friend."

I hesitated and then moved away. He spun her around quickly, and backed with her to the door. Just as he moved backward into the hallway, after a quick glance behind him, the sharp sound of the shot rang in the hall. Tram dropped like a sackful of water. Barney Zeck appeared, dusty and apologetic, a spaniel frown on his face.

"Guess I was a little hasty, maybe," he said uncertainly. "Had to get the spinal cord. Any other way and the spasm makes him yank the trigger."

Chapter Eighteen

I SLEPT until noon, got up and took another shower, hacked off the beard, and dressed in fresh clothes. The temporary relief of the rain hadn't lasted long. The thick heavy heat had spread itself over the city again, like a fat woman face down on a mudbank.

I took the phone from behind the drapery and phoned the hospital. It took them fifteen minutes to find out that she was in the process of being discharged. I told them to tell her I'd be over to pick her up.

I went over in a cab and told the driver to wait. Jill was standing at the desk, writing a check.

"Have a nice sleep, honey?" I asked.

She turned toward me. She had had a nice sleep. She looked glowing, and very lovely. I walked her out to the cab.

She got in. "Damn," she said.

"What's the trouble?"

"I could have had a by-line. Instead of pounding a typewriter, where was I? In a hospital, pounding my ear, full of sleeping pills. Great! Work your heart out for a yarn and somebody else writes it."

"You're cute as hell when you're mad," I said.

"Oh, be quiet."

"Do we just ride and ride?" the driver asked.

I gave him the name of the big air-conditioned restaurant, the same place I had walked out of, leaving Jill behind, a million years ago.

We got a booth after a short wait, and ordered two big steaks.

"Give you much trouble yesterday?" she asked.

"Oh, they kept me around until I was groggy. Dictating statements, signing them. It was a busy place. Immigration gets a bunch of aliens to deport."

"I still have that to face. But I'm rested up now."

She made a low growl as the steak was placed in front of her. As she started to cut it, I said, "Nothing annoys me more than secrecy. Phony secrecy. In your file you wrote something about Laura and the party being dangerous. I didn't know which party you meant until I found out you'd tipped them about Tram some time ago."

She worked on the steak for a while. "There's nothing I hate worse than somebody digging around in my personal papers."

"*Touché!* I was looking for cigarettes. Anyway, I told Tram about the file. That's why you had callers. I guess he had to know what was in it."

"I had callers because I said too much over the phone to someone who sounded like you. The file had nothing to do with it."

"All right. We'll call that point a draw. Even all around. Point number two. Why didn't you tell me you saw Tram coming from Laura's apartment that night?"

She gave me a wide-eyed stare, a bland stare. "But I didn't! I sensed a bluff, so I raised the pot."

"And nearly got yourself clobbered."

She grinned. "Ever hear about tattletale gray? You should have seen your face as Tram was marching me out."

"You were a nice color too. Like avocado meat."

"Something I didn't eat, no doubt."

"Look, I want to talk about something. About that note you left for me."

"There's nothing to say, Dil. Nothing at all. We were two weary people. And weary people make mistakes. Just skip it." She looked down at her plate.

"Look at me, Jill."

"You bother me. Let me eat."

"Look at me."

Her eyes came up defiantly.

"Now tell me, slowly and distinctly, to stay out of your life," I said.

"Stay—st—" She snatched up her napkin and buried her eyes in it. "That isn't a fair thing to do," she said, her voice muffled.

"You can't say it," I said.

The napkin dropped into her lap. She lifted her chin. Her gray eyes didn't see me. "Go away, Dillon Bryant, and stay out of my life. I mean it."

I got up and got out of there. How wrong can you get? I went to see Sam. I went back onto the payroll, officially. He said to pick up the plane tickets the next afternoon. He said he'd wire Paul right away. Sam tried to ask me some questions. I didn't feel like answering them, and told him so.

"Engineers!" he said with rumbling disgust. "For Chrissake, I'd rather run a chicken farm."

I decided to be taken drunk, but the second one stuck in my throat. I did a lot of walking. It felt funny to walk around the city and have nobody interested in me, feel no eyes boring into that spot between my shoulder blades.

The federal people had chased the reporters away. Everybody had the same answer. No comment. Smith was the pigeon for murders two and three. Widdmar was elected for the first one, Laura. It was a tired, hot, aimless, empty city, and the only thing ahead of me was a lot of work south of the border. I had to do something about Laura's money. Some lawyer had been trying to get hold of me.

At about five o'clock I began to get mad. It took a funny form, that anger. It transmuted itself into a couple of bottles in one bag, and a bunch of groceries in the other. There was a shining new lock on Jill's door.

Her eye appeared at the peephole. "What do you want?" she demanded.

"Refuge. I'm being pursued."

After long seconds the door opened. I pushed it open the rest of the way and went by her. I walked into the kitchen and put the stuff on the shelf. She stood behind me. She wore a print housecoat. Very severe. When I turned, she looked angry.

"Well?"

"Go out and sit. Turn on the fountain. I'm mixing a drink."

She shrugged and left the kitchen. Things were definitely cool. There were faint blue patches under her eyes. She looked as though she had been weeping.

I brought out her drink and mine and sat down expansively. "Cozy here."

"Isn't it," she said.

"The international situation still looks rough."

"It certainly does."

"Funny shape for a little birthmark, isn't it?"

"Damn you, Dillon Bryant!"

We sat in a stiff silence, sipping the drinks from time to time. I got up and made some more and brought them back.

"What do you want?" she demanded.

"Don't make me answer that. It'll spoil my technique."

"Don't you try to kiss me again. I mean that."

"I don't intend to try, thank you."

The sun was at last too low to reach into the court.

Blue shadows began to gather. She was getting more nervous by the minute.

"What *do* you want?" she demanded.

"My goodness! Why can't you just be a hostess?"

After the third round I went over and made myself comfortable on the couch. She paced back and forth as on a previous night. She hung a cigarette in the corner of her mouth, popped the kitchen match on her thumbnail, and took a kick at the leg of the coffee table. She trailed smoke after her. I laced my hands behind my head and smiled at her most amiably.

She stopped by the couch, staring down at me. "You—you—"

"Louse? Creep? You think of a good word."

She looked down at me and her face crumpled up, like the face of a child whose temper has been tried past endurance, right up to the point of tears. She fell onto my chest hard enough to drive the wind out of me. She hammered at me with one fist, her face buried in my neck. I held her and let the storm blow itself out. It did, at last, and became nothing more than dry, infrequent hiccups.

She lay still, breathing softly. I got one hand under her chin, lifted her head, pulled her up a bit, and fitted her mouth down over mine. She held her lips tightly together. And I felt that she was holding her breath.

At last she sighed against my mouth and her lips went warm and slack, like the lips of a sleepy child, parting slightly. I found the concavity of the small of her back and stroked it gently. Something new came into her lips, into her body, into her breathing. Her arms tightened and urgency came over her and she came astonishingly alive.

She lifted her head quickly, her eyes lambent. "Hey!" she said. She dipped her lips for more.

I sat up and placed her gently on the couch at arm's length. Her eyes were heavy-lidded, her head like a flower on a stalk, too heavy for the stalk.

"Busted spring?"

"Completely," she breathed.

I stood up. "Ice gone?"

"All of a sudden," she whispered.

"This we do right. This we do in a traditional way, even

to the ring. I'm leaving tomorrow. Give yourself time."

"I don't need time. I don't want time."

"I want you to have some anticipation. Look, I can finish up with Harrigan in a month. And when I come back here, I want to take you with me onto the next job."

I walked toward the door. She came after me. "Dil! The food you brought! Dil, don't leave me!"

Oh, I was a strong-minded character, all right. I left. I got out on the sidewalk and it took me ten minutes to get ten steps from the front door. I thought I had the right answer. I thought I had the right way to do it. Back in the place I would always think of as Laura's apartment, I let the phone ring and ring. I paced and smoked and paced some more. I wanted to punch holes in the wall. When the knock came on the door, I opened it.

She even remembered to bring over the groceries.

>>> If you've enjoyed this book and would like to discover more great vintage crime and thriller titles, as well as the most exciting crime and thriller authors writing today, visit: >>>

The Murder Room
Where Criminal Minds Meet

themurderroom.com